Edited by Hot Tree Editing

 This is a work of fiction. Names, characters, places and incidents are either the product of the author's imagination, or are used in a fictitious manner. Any resemblance to actual persons, living or dead, or actual events is entirely coincidental.

First Published 2026

ISBN 13: 978-1-971653-01-3

Playing for Keeps

Shatter the Ice

Book 1

MariaLisa deMora

DEDICATION

"Every day is a great day for hockey" ~ Mario Lemieux

For the Fort Wayne Komets, a gutsy team that always plays a full 60 minutes. #LetsGoKomets

CONTENTS

ACKNOWLEDGMENTS

Hockey has been part of my life for decades, starting back in the 1980s in southern Wisconsin.

When I moved to NE Indiana, it didn't take me long to find the Fort Wayne Komets, the local ECHL team. I went to several games, picking seats around the arena until I found my favorite spot, right on the glass behind the bench. That became my home during hockey season for years. When I tell you that I've had hundreds of hours of entertainment by the Komets, I'm not exaggerating.

I'd originally intended Morgan for a different series, but once I got in and really started working on his story, it had to be hockey. Once I made that determination, the story flowed so fast I'd spend long hours writing. Then he decided to have more than one story, so we get three.

This is the first book in my new "Shatter the Ice" series. These books were driven first by Morgan being chatty, but also by me missing hockey. After acquiring a TBI, even two years past the event, I still can't go to an arena. So I adjusted, and I now watch every Komets game on streaming, so I still get my hockey fix.

Hope you get your fix from this book!

#hockeyfan4life

Woofully yours,
~ML

PLAYING FOR KEEPS

He's the league's quiet defenseman with a secret that could destroy everything. Morgan Oakson is one shift away from the Cup...and one bruise away from breaking. Behind closed doors, his boyfriend Burke controls every breath, every dollar, every truth Morgan dares not speak. That he's gay, and that the man who claims to love him also promises to ruin him.

When a desperate 911 call goes wrong, the one person who sees through Morgan's lies is the last person he expected, his openly gay coach, Marshall Davies. One business card. One promise. One chance to escape before the next fist lands.

In a world that punishes vulnerability with a slash to the throat, Morgan will have to decide what's worth fighting for. The Cup, his life, or the terrifying possibility of being loved exactly as he is.

Raw, heart-pounding, and unapologetically queer, *Playing for Keeps* is a gripping hurt/comfort sports romance about surviving the unthinkable, and discovering that the hardest hits don't always happen on the ice.

Chapter One

The door clicked shut, a soft sound that echoed like a slapshot in Morgan Oakson's ears. He slumped back against the bathroom door, shoulders sliding down the wood until the cold tile floor met his ass and halted his descent. He didn't dare lock the door. His phone trembled in his hand, the screen glowing with the pre-entered digits for 911. His thumb hovered over the green Call button, heart hammering so loud, he swore it could wake the city.

Blood crusted his temple, skin still stinging around where it was matted in his hair, and his playoff beard also itched with drying red. He pressed his palm to his other ear, blocking out the creak of floorboards beyond the door. With a shaky finger, he tapped the icon.

"911, what's your emergency?" The operator's voice was sharp, slicing through the quiet. Morgan flinched, pressing the phone tighter to his ear, terrified Burke might hear.

"What's the address of your emergency?" she pressed.

Morgan swallowed, throat tight as if filled with lead. "I...uh...I'd like to order a pizza, please." He winced. The code phrase felt childish, and his whispering voice quavered with a level of desperate need he didn't recognize. He waited for a response, pulse thundering.

"This is 911. This line is for emergencies only." Her tone hardened, becoming impatient.

"Yes, thank you." Morgan steadied himself, the quiver in his voice fading. "Pepperoni, please. The address is—"

"Do you think this is a joke?" the operator snapped. "Think domestic violence is funny? There's no reason to tie up an emergency line, mocking people who need help. I'm sure you and your friends saw some social media video and thought you'd get some kicks out of pretending you're battered. Not today. Not on my line." Her voice rose to a shout, then silence.

Morgan turned the phone to see the screen glaring "Call Ended." Defeat sank into his bones, heavier than the bruises blooming across his face. It had been a long shot, but it was now only a whiffed chance, like a one-timer from the blue line that sailed wide of an open net. He pushed off the floor, legs unsteady, and faced the cracked mirror above the sink.

That reflection was brutally honest about his situation. A broad swath of blood had smeared across his cheek, and his eye, already turning black, was rapidly swelling, while his hair was matted over one ear. His playoff beard, barely grown, glistened with red streaks.

Dropping his gaze, he noticed the phone case was smeared with crimson fingerprints. He scrubbed it clean with a damp cloth, silenced it, and shoved the device into his pocket. Morgan turned on the faucet and didn't bother waiting for warm water. Soap and water burned as he washed the blood away, dabbing at cuts with careful fingers, and slowly applied tape strips from the cabinet. He knew he would be able to hide a lot of the damage. The black eye, though—there'd be no hiding that. *That's tomorrow's problem*, he thought, shaking his head.

"Babe?" Burke's voice slithered through the door, the opening notes of his way too familiar "I'm sorry" routine.

Morgan's nose, already very swollen, forced him to open his mouth for a deep breath. He held it for five seconds, then exhaled slowly. *Time to keep the peace*. Another outburst now, so soon after feeling Burke's fists, could mean real injury on the near horizon. He might wind up with broken ribs, maybe worse. He couldn't risk that. Not with the team counting on him for the playoffs.

He pulled the door open, forcing himself to smile at the dark-haired man in the doorway. "Yeah? Just needed to take a piss." Burke would know the lie, but it was expected, and with a nod it became an entry into Burke-approved dialogue for the "after." The less Morgan acknowledged the violence, the sooner it could fade into the past. He needed to change the topic, and fast. "What do you feel like for supper? I could cook, or we can order in?"

"Baby." Burke's hand cupped Morgan's jaw, the touch cold despite the warmth of his fingers. He rose on his toes, pressing hard lips against Morgan's painfully swollen ones. "Let's order in. I want you to take it easy. You've got a big game Saturday."

"Okay." Morgan's breath hitched, not from desire but revulsion, a reflex he couldn't fully mask. It hadn't been desire for over a year, not since Burke's charm turned to control. "Any preference on food?"

"Whatever you want, babe." Burke's quick return to pet names meant the bruises probably looked worse than Morgan had thought.

"Thai?" Morgan offered Burke's favorite, ducking when Burke lifted his hand again. His fingers trailed along the side of Morgan's face as he turned away. "I'll call it in."

He dug out his phone, pausing at the call log. There were two missed calls from an unknown number above the failed 911 attempt. With quick swipes, he deleted all three, erasing the evidence. Then he ordered Burke's usual pad Thai and a mild soup for himself, his stomach too nerve-churned for more.

Twenty minutes later, the delivery arrived. Morgan plated Burke's food and carried it to the couch, where Burke sprawled, eyes on the TV. "The soup will be messy, so I'm eating in the kitchen," Morgan mumbled, tensing as Burke's hand clamped onto his.

"Oh, babe. I really messed up this time, didn't I?" Burke took the plate and set it on the coffee table, standing too close, his exhalation hot on Morgan's neck. "I'm sorry. I wish you didn't make me so mad. You know how I get." He gripped the back of Morgan's neck, yanking him down with a jerk. Burke whispered, "If you'd just stop making me mad, we wouldn't have these problems. You know what my options are." He paused, then finished with a sarcastic, "Babe."

The problem was that Morgan hadn't done anything. He'd walked in from practice, exhausted, and Burke's rage, fueled by another gambling loss, had erupted. Money was almost always the trigger. The other option he'd referred to was the ever-present threat to out Morgan as queer.

Morgan fixed his gaze on Burke's ear, avoiding his eyes. "It's okay. I understand," he lied, voice flat.

"If you'd give me a card on the account, we wouldn't need to talk about money." Burke shook his head, feigning sadness. "You bring this on yourself, being so suspicious. It's like you don't trust me."

"The bank needs an in-person visit to add a signature." A convenient truth, one Morgan clung to. He shrugged, wincing as pain flared in his ribs.

Burke's jaw ticked, a vein pulsing at his temple. "If you'd switch to a bank that was close by, it wouldn't be an issue. This kinda feels intentional," Burke said, voice tight. "You know I don't like when you don't trust me."

Morgan's pulse spiked. This could spiral fast. He needed to find a solution. "I'll hit the ATM tomorrow, get some cash?" he offered, knowing the $200 daily limit was his shield. "Then you can watch the ponies run?"

Burke's eyes softened, a predator's satisfaction. "Good boy."

Morgan nodded, retreating to the kitchen and his soup, the lie of normalcy settling like ash in his mouth. He was about halfway through the soup when it happened again.

"Fucking hell, I was going to bet parlay on that race." The shout came from the living room, followed by the stomp of Burke's feet aimed towards the kitchen. Morgan froze. "Fucking useless moron. I'd have made bank."

CHAPTER TWO

Morgan grimaced, pausing in the hallway outside Coach Marshall Davies' office. The summons had come mid-stride, via a teammate's nudge and a pointed "Hey, Coach wants you." His face throbbed, the black eye now in full dark purple bloom, impossible to hide. He forced a lopsided smile and stepped into the doorway.

"Hey, Coach. You know how clumsy I am off the ice. I fell." The lie tasted sour, one he'd peddled too often this year. "I'm good to play for Saturday, though. Raring to go."

Marshall Davies loomed behind his desk, a mountain of a man at six foot four, his broad frame dwarfing Morgan's six one. Fifteen years past his playing days, he hadn't lost the bulk or the sharp gaze that sized up a situation in a heartbeat. His eyes roamed Morgan's face, lingering on the bruises, then dropped to his wrists, where the compression shirt peeked out. The end of May was no time for layers, and they both knew it.

"Come in." Coach's head tipped towards the chairs. "Close the door."

Shit. Shit, shit, shit. Morgan's stomach churned. "I'm good to play Saturday, promise."

Coach's gaze didn't waver, his head tipping towards the door this time, silent command clear. Morgan complied. He shut the door and sank into the chair, ignoring the aching stab in his side courtesy of the televised race results from last night. Burke's fists had found their favorite mark again.

"Door's closed, just you and me, Morgan," Coach said, voice low, a mix of tenderness and steel that raised the hair on Morgan's neck. "What gets said in here stays in here. No judgment from me. You know I'm gay."

Morgan nodded slowly, dread pooling in his gut. Coach had come out when he shifted from playing to coaching, a bold move that had cost him his first job offer but landed him here. If anyone understood the closet's weight in terms of hockey, it was him.

"If one of my players got bashed at a club, I'd ask them to report it," Coach continued, sidestepping Morgan's unspoken truth. "For their sake, and for the next guy's."

"It's nothing like that, Coach." Morgan's eyes dropped to his knees, the worn denim a safe anchor as he lied to the one man he trusted. "I fell."

"Pull your shirt up, Morgan." Coach leaned forwards, elbows on the desk. "Show me your torso and tell me you fell. I bet those bruises aren't as old as the ones on your face. They never are. Once a bully sees evidence of their actions, they'll switch to the ones easier to hide."

Morgan froze, teeth clenching. Pain pulsed in his jaw. "I'd rather not, Coach. Sir."

“I bet.” Silence stretched, sending Morgan’s heart racing. “Did you know I volunteer?”

“Sir?” Morgan blinked, thrown by the shift.

“Volunteer. Donating time, no pay. It’s a whole thing, Oakson.”

Morgan exhaled, hoping the first-name moment had passed. “I know what volunteering is. Didn’t know you did it.”

“Yeah. At the YMCA, for their LGBTQ+ program. It’s for kids whose parents don’t know they’re on some part of the Kinsey scale, those needing to stay closeted for family or academic career.” Coach’s voice softened. “Like me, back in the day. I used every excuse in the book for my injuries. I was always falling, or I was clumsy, or caught a puck to the face during unauthorized practice, tripped on my own feet. If there’s a lexicon, I’m sure I hit every entry. Lies, all of them. I’m not sure the balance sheet evens out, even now. Me coming out cost me family, friends...and a lot of teammates that I’ll never speak to again. It wasn’t easy. Not at all. But it’s been totally worth it to get to live my truth. Because of that, I don’t tally the losses often.”

Morgan gripped his jeans, fingers digging into the seams. Coach’s excuses of clumsiness, falling, catching a puck...they all directly mirrored his own.

"I also volunteer at a domestic abuse hotline," Coach said. "Folks mostly call when they've turned the corner towards hopeless, not really expecting anything to change. But it can." He opened a drawer, pulling out a business card. "Last night, you called 911. The pizza thing?"

"What?" Morgan's eyes squeezed shut, betrayal by his own mouth. *In for a penny.* "She laughed. Well, didn't laugh, but chewed me out for wasting time. Said I was mocking real victims. I couldn't argue with her. Couldn't explain. He might've been right outside the door."

"I figured as much when her supervisor forwarded me the call recording. We coordinate with the 911 call center and have folks in place to try and intercept those kind of calls. Ones that might go unrecognized by some of the operators."

"I didn't know what to do." Morgan hated that he was near tears. He cleared his throat. "It was a bad night, but I got by."

"You know, with your size, guys on the ice expect you to be a brawler," Coach said. "But you skate away. You're there to play, not fight. I'd bet it's the same when you're at home, that you don't usually fight back. You take it, let it be done."

Morgan nodded, throat tight. "There'd be consequences if I didn't."

"I bet. Just like larger doesn't mean aggressive, someone being smaller doesn't mean they're weaker. Not when we're looking at abuse," Coach said, sliding the card across the desk. "Emotional, physical, all that shit, it can come from anywhere. This is the hotline where I volunteer. It's an intentionally easy number to remember. There's a foundation tied to it, and we do extractions, source legal help, even involve police when needed, all private, all very discreet. If you can't keep the card, memorize the number. Promise you'll call when you need to."

Morgan stood, taking the card, ignoring the heat where Coach's fingers brushed his. "I will." He studied the card: *Hurt No More*. "I get it. I promise, Coach."

***

Marshall

Marshall stayed at his desk long after Morgan left, the kid's bruised face burned into his mind. The glimpse in the hallway of Morgan's fingers probing his side had screamed trouble. Marshall knew the signs. Hell, he'd been one who tested his own pain limits too many times in his playing days. Not from a boyfriend, but from careless hookups in dive bars before apps made finding like-minded men safer. He remembered one time when the guy delivered a hammer blow while his cock was still in Marshall's mouth. *Physics wasn't the dude's strong suit.* He snorted. *I nearly sheared the manhood off him.*

His volunteering with the hotline wasn't about his past but his sister's. If Dottie had access to a hotline, maybe she'd still be here, not reduced to a gravestone he couldn't face. It had been nearly fifteen years, and he still couldn't accept it. Maybe if he'd been around more, he might have seen what was going on. Her boyfriend had been vicious on the ice, but Dottie had told Marshall more than once that he wasn't like that at home. *Lies.*

He shook his head, forcing his focus back to the roster on his desk. Playoff changes were a grind, but only one loss stood between them and an exit. Win, and they were still in the hunt. Lose, and it was golf tee times for all.

It had been hard enough keeping his mind on the necessary changes before talking to Morgan. He had a deal cooking, and the potential change in his personal situation rode the edge of his consciousness, all day, every day. He hoped he'd hear from his agent today. It would be nice to have the new offer buttoned up before the season ended, whether tomorrow or after the finals.

Marshall shook his head, dragging the paperwork back in front of him.

Morgan's name stared back at him, unblemished on paper but so badly bruised in reality. Marshall's gut twisted, knowing he shouldn't pull him without proof, not this far into the playoffs, not the way the kid had been playing.

Not without pulling out a miracle.

CHAPTER THREE

Morgan

Morgan's hands shook as he tucked the hotline card back into his wallet, wedging it behind his driver's license where Burke wouldn't look. The bathroom mirror reflected the same battered face, but the card's weight in his pocket felt like a lifeline, fragile as it was. The house was quiet, a silence that felt too solemn. It was middle of the afternoon, and Burke had just left for the track, his mood buoyed by Morgan's delivery of ATM cash, but the silence didn't soothe. It prickled, like the calm before a savage hit on the ice.

Morgan wandered into the kitchen, the linoleum cool under his bare feet. He opened the fridge and stared at the half-empty shelves—ketchup, a wilted lettuce head, a six-pack of Burke's cheap beer. Nothing nutritional like what was needed as fuel at this point in the playoffs. His stomach growled, but the thought of food twisted it further.

Instead, he grabbed a glass from the cupboard, the one with a faded hockey logo, a gift from a fan after his rookie season. After filling it with tap water, he sipped slowly, the cool water soothing his swollen lips.

Outside, a neighbor's dog barked, a normal sound that felt foreign in this apartment. He set the glass down, the clink loud in the silence, and glanced at the clock.

Two hours until Burke might return. Two hours to decide his life.

He picked up Burke's half-eaten pad Thai from last night and scraped the leftovers in the trash and then put it in the sink next to his bowl and spoon.

He wandered back into the living room and sank onto the couch, dishes forgotten in the kitchen. Morgan stared at his phone. The hotline number glared from the card in his mind, now memorized. *Hurt No More*. Three words that promised too much.

His thumb hovered over the keypad, heart thudding. What if Burke came back early? What if the operator dismissed him again? The 911 call still stung, the woman's voice echoing with her dismissive "Not on my line." But Coach's voice cut through the fear. *"Promise you'll call."* Morgan's chest hitched with a held-in sob, and once he got himself under control, he dialed.

"Hotline, this is Sarah." The voice was calm, steady, not like the 911 operator's edge. "How can I help you?"

Morgan's throat tightened. "I need help. My boyfriend, um, he's…" The words stuck, heavy as the bruises on his ribs. "He hits me. I tried 911, used the pizza thing, but they hung up."

"I'm so sorry that happened," Sarah said, no judgment in her tone. "You're safe to talk to me, I promise. Can you tell me where you are? Are you in danger?"

"Not right now. He's out, at the races." Morgan's eyes darted to the door, half expecting Burke was going to burst into the apartment. "I'm out north of town. But he'll be back tonight. It's...it's been bad lately. So bad. Money sets him off."

Sarah's voice stayed steady, guiding him through several questions. How long? How severe? Any weapons in the house?

Morgan answered in fragments, shame mixing with a heady relief. Burke's gambling losses, the fists, the threats to out him as the "first gay hockey player."

Sarah listened, then outlined a plan. She promised him a safe place to stay, police escort if needed, and legal aid. "We can get you out today if you're ready. Can you pack a bag?"

Morgan's gaze fell to the coffee table, for the first time seeing a smear of blood where Burke's half-eaten pad Thai had been. His ribs ached with every breath, a reminder of last night's second "lesson." "Yeah, totally," he whispered. "I'm ready."

Chapter Four

Marshall

Marshall sat at his kitchen table, a half-eaten sandwich in front of him. The radio hummed a classic rock tune set low enough not to drown out the bustle of the city outside his apartment window. He flipped through a sports magazine, lingering on a feature about queer athletes.

A photo of a smiling rugby player caught his eye, the athlete out and proud, something he'd never dared or aspired to as a player. It had been hard enough coming out after his playing career was over. And didn't that memory make him wince. The illegal slash that took out his knee, the wounded face of his surgeon. Marshall had found out later he was a hockey fan.

His sister's face flashed in his mind. It was always the intangible things that caught him off guard, like Dottie's laugh and her stubborn streak. He reached for his coffee mug, the ceramic warm against his palm, and took a sip, grimacing at the bitter dregs.

The clock ticked past seven o'clock, another long day at the rink behind him. Game tomorrow. He felt like the boys were as prepared as he could make them. Only the scoreboard would tell if he'd pulled seven nationalities, five languages, and twenty-two men onto the same page.

He stood to rinse the mug, heard a distinct beep, and glanced at his phone, the hotline app glowing. He answered on instinct, years of volunteering kicking in. "Hotline, this is Marshall."

"Hi."

The voice on the other end was muffled, hesitant, but the fear was familiar enough to make his gut clench.

"Can you tell me what's happening?"

"It's...so hard." The caller's voice broke during a shaky exhale. "My dad hits me. He hates me. Hates that I'm gay. I tried 911 but hung up. I was too scared. Wasn't sure if they were in Dad's precinct. I'm eighteen, but I don't know what to do. Don't you think I should know what to do?"

Marshall leaned forwards, pen poised over a notepad, forcing his voice to stay calm. "You're doing the right thing by calling. Are you safe now? Where are you?" The words felt mechanical, but his mind raced. That voice was rough, low, and raw, just like someone he'd seen limping through the team's halls.

"Winnebago County, out in the country. He's at work for another couple hours. I...I can't keep doing this." A pause, then, quieter, he continued, "He threatens to kill me sometimes. I don't know what to do. What would be easier."

Marshall's pen froze. He didn't say it. Couldn't. Couldn't talk about his sister. Protocol demanded neutrality, but his pulse spiked. "Okay, here's what we offer. We can get you to a safe place. Can you pack? Just a small bag, but put all your important papers in. Don't forget any cash you have stashed. We'll send someone, but I'm thinking we don't want to tag the police as an escort, not given your family situation, but it'll still be discreet and very safe." He scribbled notes, then typed in the information to coordinate with their extraction team. The kid would be taken to a safe house in nearby suburbs using a civilian car, and they'd have a lawyer on standby for a restraining order. "We can stay on the line until they're close. As long as you want. Can you do that?"

"Yeah." The voice steadied, a flicker of resolve. "I'm Greg." A sob broke through. "I'm Greg."

Marshall's chest tightened, but he kept his tone even. "Greg, I'm here until you're safe." He put the call on speaker and stayed on while he organized the rescue, guiding Greg through packing, advising him to bring the essentials only, no trace left for his dad to follow. The extraction crew were enroute, about ten minutes out.

Marshall's mind churned with distractions because Morgan, his player, was hiding something like this. He pushed down the urge to drive there himself, focusing on the call until Greg confirmed the team was at the door.

***

Morgan

The knock came soft but firm, like a ref's whistle cutting through chaos. Morgan peered through the peephole and saw two plainclothes officers, badges glinting on their belts. He opened the door, duffel bag already slung over his shoulder, heart pounding.

"Morgan Oakson?" the woman asked, voice low.

He nodded, glancing down the hallway for Burke. *Nothing. I'm safe now.*

They led him to an unmarked sedan, the male officer scanning the apartment building as they moved.

"The foundation has organized a place for you," the woman said, sliding into the driver's seat. "Safe house, about twenty minutes out. You'll meet a counselor there."

Morgan sank into the backseat, the duffel heavy on his lap. The city blurred past, streetlights streaking like missed shots.

The next game of the playoff round was tomorrow night. They were down three games to two, which meant this game would be a do-or-die. They had to win to stay in the race. Miss the mark, and everyone on the team would be going home much earlier than they wanted.

The safe house was a nondescript bungalow tucked into a quiet suburb. Inside, the promised counselor named Lisa waited, her smile gentle but not pitying. “You’ve already done the hardest part,” she said, guiding him to a couch. “Getting out.”

Morgan’s throat burned as he recounted the last year with Burke, the most embarrassing part of it that he was a hookup turned jailer, threats piling up like penalties. Lisa listened, jotting notes, then outlined next steps he should prepare for, including therapy, a restraining order, ending the lease on the car, and definitely breaking the lease on the apartment to get a new place. “You’re not alone in this,” she said.

***

Marshall

“Kid was scared to death.” Marshall blew out a hard sigh. “Did you get him to the safe house without issue?”

Karen from the extraction team nodded. “Yeah. We got him out of there just in time. Saw his old man’s car coming in on our drive out. Greg was reported as missing about thirty minutes later. He’s already talked to the judge about a restraining order.” She leaned back in Marshall’s kitchen chair, coffee in a mug in front of her. “Good kid. His family lotto just sucked.”

“Will there be any issues for the foundation?”

“Shouldn’t be, even if the old man has access to the kid’s phone records. The calls come to a randomized number aliased to whoever is next in the rotation for a chat, and at three rings, it rolls to whoever is next after that. There's nothing to pin that number on the hotline." She would know. She'd been the one who set everything up years ago.

"Good. That's good."

"He's also a low-level cop, whose anger problem extends to work, apparently."

He shrugged. "That'll make getting the restraining order easier."

"Yeah. Oh, hey, you missed out on a call, though. Sarah took the one in front of yours, and it turned out the kid is a hockey player. Terrified young man. I thought you'd know him." She tipped her head to one side. "Isn't it a coincidence that he plays on your team and called your hotline? Huh."

"I gave him a card earlier in the day. I'm glad he found the courage to make the call." Marshall blew out another breath, feeling something ease in his chest, a tightness he hadn't known he carried. He repeated, "I'm glad he called."

***

Morgan

Morgan's phone buzzed again, this time with a text from an unknown number.

It's Marshall. Hotline coordinator gave me the address if you need anything. Can I stop by briefly? Just to check in.

His thumb hovered over the reply. Part of him wanted to say no, to curl up in this anonymous room and hide. But Coach had been the one to hand him that card. His was the one voice that had cut through the fog. *Sure,* he typed back. *Come on by.*

Fifteen minutes later, a soft knock echoed through the bungalow. Morgan opened the door to find Marshall standing there, not in his coaching team-logo gear but in a simple hoodie and jeans, holding two takeout coffees. His broad frame filled the doorway, but his expression was soft, almost tentative.

"Figured you might need this," Marshall said, handing over a cup. "Black, no sugar. Lisa said it was okay for me to drop by. Volunteer rules and all."

Morgan nodded, stepping aside to let him in. They settled at the small kitchen table, the steam from the coffee curling between them like a fragile bridge. The safe house was quiet, save for the distant hum of a neighbor's mower outside.

"I don't know what to say," Morgan admitted, staring into his cup. "One minute I'm ordering Thai to keep the peace, the next I'm here, with nothing but a duffel. I'm off-balance. Feels like I'm broken. Like Burke smashed something in me that won't fix."

Marshall's eyes met his, steady and unflinching. "You're not broken, Morgan. Bruised, yeah. But I've seen guys come back from worse on the ice—and off it. My sister, she went through something similar. She had a controlling boyfriend, the kind who made her doubt every move. She hid it for years, like you did. I wish I'd seen the signs sooner." His voice cracked just a fraction, but he cleared his throat. "Point is, calling that hotline? That was you fighting back. That's strength."

Morgan's chest tightened, a mix of grief and relief washing over him. No one had ever looked at him like this—not with pity, but with understanding, like they saw the fighter beneath the discolored skin. Their eyes locked for a long moment, the air thickening with an unspoken connection.

Marshall's hand twitched on the table, as if he wanted to reach out, but he didn't. Instead, he just nodded. "You're going to be okay. Better than okay."

Morgan exhaled, the weight on his shoulders lifted just a bit. "Thanks, Coach. Marshall. For seeing that."

Marshall stood, giving him space. "Anytime. Get some rest. You've got a fresh start waiting." He left, the door locking softly behind him, but the warmth of his presence lingered, a quiet promise amid the chaos.

Later, Morgan sat on the narrow bed, the mattress creaking under his weight. The room was sparse—a lamp, a dresser, a window with blinds.

He unzipped his duffel and pulled out a worn jersey, the number 17 faded from too many washes. It was from his junior league days, back when the game of hockey was still an escape, not ever-escalating pressure. He held it to his chest, the fabric soft. He imagined it still smelling of rink and sweat.

Outside, barely-there music played from somewhere distant, and out-too-late kids laughed from down the street. Normal, but everything sounded alien now. He lay back, staring at the ceiling, the jersey draped over him like a shield. And for the first time in months, he slept through the night undisturbed.

CHAPTER FIVE

Marshall

Marshall paced the team's office, roster sheets ignored on his desk. The brief visit with Morgan last night had gutted him. It wasn't just knowing Morgan'd had to handle so much abuse, but the level of fear that was still in his voice, as if the safe house was a haven that could be stripped away.

He'd had an idea after leaving the safe house last night.

So, he'd been at work since before dawn, talking to Morgan's agent and then team management as he pushed for a trade, citing the "potential" of a rival team's second-rate blueliner to the management. All while still preparing for the game.

Now, the trade was in motion. The only thing holding it up was papers awaiting signatures. It'd get Morgan out of the city and move him cleanly away from Burke's reach. As far as he was concerned, Marshall's own deal was taking back burner to this one.

His phone pinged with a text from the foundation coordinator confirming Greg's restraining order had been signed by a judge. Marshall exhaled, but that relief was short-lived. He couldn't get away from thinking about Morgan. Feelings still stirred, completely unprofessional ones. If he closed his eyes, he could still see Morgan's broad shoulders, the way his eyes had met Marshall's over that little table, full of secrets he was terrified to reveal.

Don't go there, Marshall warned himself. For now, at least, he was just Coach, not a savior. It was crazy, but this urge to protect Morgan, to be more than a mentor, gnawed at him.

He met with the GM, doing his best to sell the trade as a strategic move. "Knell's got untapped grit," he said, leaning on the stats of the acquisition to mask his real motive.

The GM nodded and signed off on the terms of the trade. Marshall's chest loosened slightly. With this trade, Morgan would be safe—physically, at least. He'd be out of reach from his abusive ex. But the emotional tangle, the spark Marshall had felt when their fingers brushed over that card? That was a problem for another day.

***

Morgan

"No, no. Gary, I know I should have told you." Morgan sighed. "Do we have to go over this now? What's going on?"

Gary Thomas, his agent and manager of both his sports career and now, apparently, his personal life, too, sighed bigger than Morgan had. "You've got to give me a minute to get caught up. I had no idea you'd moved a guy into your—"

"I didn't. He moved himself in with threats and fear."

"—that a guy had moved himself into your apartment. I've been to your apartment and never saw anyone. Certainly not a *guy*."

"It's been nearly two years since you last visited, Gary."

"No, I was there last year. Wasn't I? I know we had a face-to-face meeting. At least one."

"You came to Florida year before last for a road trip and spent nearly half our meeting talking about your sunburn and slathering on some facial cream that honestly smelled weird."

"He wasn't there, right?"

"No, he never traveled with me. Not because he didn't try, but because it was the one line I wouldn't back down from."

"Probably a smart line to hold, kiddo." Gary sighed again. "I'm glad you called this morning. The GM reached out today. I was glad I knew what was going on personally before I talked to the big dog."

"Oh, that's never a good thing. Am I traded?" He was almost joking, but in an industry where players were simply assets, it was always a threat.

"Yeah, kiddo. But it's a really good offer. They sold your rights to the Dingoes." He could hear the wince in Gary's voice. "With a two-way contract, it was either the Dingoes, or they'd bump you down two levels. I don't want to see you clawing back to relevancy from the basement of the minors, Morgan. It's a good offer, but it's a iron fist in a velvet glove. There's no wiggle room in what we're dealing with."

"Dingoes." Morgan closed his eyes in relief. "That's half a state away."

"I know it's not a place you ever saw yourself playing."

Morgan laughed, catching it about halfway through and choking off the terrible noise. "No, you don't get it. This is the best possible option. Burke can't easily get to me there."

"Burke is probably a very angry person right now."

"Thanks for being willing to take care of the lease for me."

"Won't be hard, just a few calls. One to the agent we rented from, one to the moving company about getting your stuff into storage, and one to the police to evict one squatting dickwad."

"I appreciate you, Gary."

"You didn't even ask how much your new contract is."

"Doesn't matter. If it's a loss, it's still a good thing."

"I appreciate you, too, Morgan." His tone had changed, flooding with emotion, and Morgan squeezed his eyes closed. "I hate that I never caught on that something was wrong. I feel like I failed you. For Christ's sake, I didn't even know you were gay."

"Gary, I went out of my way to hide everything that was happening. From you, from Mom, from teammates, and from my coaches. It just all caught up with me."

"Mom. Well, hell, that's another topic. Have you told her yet?"

"What? That I'm gay? No, she'd have me kidnapped and deprogrammed before you could say evangelical conservative Christians."

"Jesus, kid. Jesus." Gary coughed. "How much danger do you think that there is of Burke the asshole finding a sports magazine to sell his story to?"

"Pretty high. We probably need to have a conversation with the PR person for the Dingoes as a first priority."

"I'll make that my fourth call, then."

"Thanks, Gary."

"I'll be in touch, kiddo."

The call disconnected, and Morgan happened to be looking at his phone when another call came in, but it flipped immediately over to voicemail. *Burke*. He'd changed settings to have all calls except from Gary roll to voicemail. One small thing he could manage on his own.

He looked around the room he'd hardly left since coming in last night. It was nice—nicer than he'd expected when Sarah had first talked about the safe house. He didn't know why he'd had a preconceived idea of what it would look like, but apparently in his imagination, safe house and flophouse were synonymous.

Morgan saw another call come in, and the icon appeared for voicemail. He threw the phone on the bed. "I'm just so tired of everything."

He explored the bruises on his face, poking hard at the most painful places as if in penance. With short sleeves on, he could see the bright bruises around each wrist where Burke had yanked him around the apartment. A fingertip survey of those rewarded him with more pain. "One good thing about being traded. I don't have to explain to the guys what happened."

He grabbed his phone and opened the text thread with Gary. *I'm going to need somewhere to live down by the Dingoes.*

Way ahead of you, kiddo. Already sourced. Saves storage for the furniture.

Thanks again, Gary.

Yup.

“If there’s any furniture left after Burke’s temper tantrum when he realized his cash cow had escaped the barn. Doesn’t matter. Everything’s replaceable.”

Morgan stretched out on the bed again, throwing an arm across his eyes and cursing softly when that reckless movement hurt like a bastard. “Face, arms, ribs. Most damage, less damage, least damage. What a thoughtful guy Burke was.”

It struck him suddenly that he didn’t have to play tonight.

Morgan blew out a long stream of air that trailed off into laughter.

“Oh, I’m going to fucking sleep for a year.”

***

Marshall

Midafternoon, Marshall stopped at a coffee shop near the arena, the kind with mismatched artsy chairs and baristas who remembered his order was a plain black, no sugar.

He sat at a table by the window, watching commuters hustle past, this tiny moment in time where their lives crossed with his in a blur of normalcy. His laptop was open to game footage, but his eyes drifted to a photo he had set as the background of the computer. It was him and his sister at a lake, her grin wide, his arm around her. He traced the edge, the surface giving slightly underneath his touch.

The barista dropped off a second order of his coffee, steam curling up, and said, “Rough day, Coach?”

Marshall shrugged, forcing a smile. “Just planning tonight’s win.” But his thoughts were on Morgan, not the game.

Chapter Six

Morgan

Morgan stepped onto his new team's ice. The suburban arena was slightly smaller but a lot brighter than the old barn. The air smelled of fresh paint and ambition, not stale sweat and old pads. His new teammates were different. A lot less cliquey, more open, tossing pucks around with easy grins. He adjusted his pads away from any tender but healing places and skated warm-up laps, testing his stride. The swiftness of the trade had been a shock, but even right now, barely a day in, it felt good, like a clean break from all the bad things Burke had brought into his life.

One of the things he hadn't counted on was the Geese winning the last game and keeping their playoff chances alive. Then there would have been a four- or five-day gap between games. But the second round wasn't done. The Dingoes should have beaten them, so either the Geese played better without him on the ice, or the blueliner traded for him had been critical to their defense. He hadn't been able to sleep like he'd promised himself, so he'd sat in the nosebleed seats, watching the game unfold in front of him, without him. A very weird three hours.

Still, overall, things went well.

Today's practice had been brutal, the coach pushing speed drills that had left Morgan gasping. He welcomed the burn because it helped drown out Burke's ghost. Off ice, teammates invited him to a bar, their banter light but probing.

"Heard you came from the big city," a winger named Jake said, eyeing Morgan's fading bruises. "Rough exit?"

Morgan shrugged, muttering about a "bad fall," but Jake's nod held no judgment.

Later, Morgan joined Jake and Riley, the goalie, at a dive bar near the rink, the kind with sticky floors and neon signs that usually served killer burgers. He nursed a ginger ale, the fizz sharp on his tongue, while his teammates downed beers, laughing about a botched play in practice.

When Jake slid a basket of fries across the table, saying, "Eat, man, you're too skinny for a D-man," Morgan snorted and grabbed a fry. The jukebox kicked on, some old Springsteen tune, and for a moment, it felt like he was just another guy, not a secret or a survivor. Just a guy sitting with people who might become friends, eating a greasy burger that tasted fantastic. He leaned back, the chatter washing over him, and let himself smile.

It wasn't until the next day that he realized the first game against his old team was inevitable. He'd planned on asking his new coach to have him be the healthy scratch, but after only two practices, he'd started clicking with Thompson, the other D-man on his line. Second line, a down move for him and an up move for Thompson. Either way, they were clicking like they'd skated together for years.

With the Dingoes now in a do-or-die for the rivalry match, each team sitting at three games won, he thought he could contribute in a positive way, so he kept his mouth shut.

By gametime the atmosphere in the rink was crackling with tension.

During warmups Morgan spotted Coach behind the Geese's bench, his broad frame unmistakable. Anger flared, but only for a moment. He'd realized Coach had to have pushed the trade. Had likely been the sole architect of Morgan moving teams. But beneath it, something else stirred, a pull Morgan couldn't name. He gripped his stick tighter, channeling it into the game. Every check, every shot, was a defiance of Burke's shadow.

***

Morgan took his place near the back of the snaking line of players to commiserate with the Geese on their season-ending loss. The Dingoes had come out of the first faceoff with three times the energy the Geese had brought to the ice.

From his seat on the bench, waiting for his time to get into the game, Morgan had watched his new team pick apart the defense of his old team. He didn't know how to feel yet. With this game the Dingoes moved into the semifinals, and with their loss, the Geese would be packing up lockers in the next couple of days, an end-of-season tradition no one enjoyed.

CHAPTER SEVEN

Marshall

The rink buzzed with rivalry energy, the Geese versus the Dingoes, Morgan's new team against his old. Marshall had stood in the management box during warmups, arms crossed, watching Morgan skate. There was a visceral change in the process for Morgan, and Marshall thought it might be joy. The kid looked like he was enjoying himself for the first time in forever.

During the game, Morgan had proven he was already a vital part of his team's chemistry, weaving through Geese defenders like they were stationary cones, his passes crisp in spite of the fading black eye and however many other lingering bruises. He and the other D-man on his line seemed to have a mental connection, reading each other's minds as they wheeled in and around the attack zone. Both defensemen on that second line had two assists by the end of the second period, and Morgan had a goal.

Marshall's chest swelled with pride, then tightened. He shouldn't allow himself to be distracted—not by these conflicting feelings. Of course he wanted the Geese to win. That would ensure them another four games at least and would give him a decent bonus for each game of the next round that his team could win.

But they didn't win. The Dingoes trounced them soundly, like he'd honestly expected at the last game. That win had been through toughness and force of will, and it seemed both features were less prominent than before—at least for the Geese.

Post game, the teams mingled in the hotel bar, tension easing into beers and mild trash talk. Tee-time jokes abounded, and Marshall watched how Morgan grinned from where he lingered at the edge, nursing a beer. He would run his guys to bed soon and give the Dingoes space to really celebrate their win tonight.

He took a sip of his beer, his gaze lingering on Morgan. The air crackled when their eyes met. Marshall nodded towards the hallway, a silent invitation he wasn't certain of even as he made it.

Morgan followed him, and in a dim alcove, words failed Marshall.

"You look good in the coach suit." Morgan flashed a grin through a split lip he had earned tonight. "I wanted to tell you thanks. For everything. But more than anything, for giving me hockey back. I didn't realize how much I resented it until I didn't anymore."

"I'm glad. You played exceptionally well tonight."

"Better than Knell, poor guy. He didn't get much ice time."

"He'll earn it next year. You were clicking with the other second liners really well."

"We'll be better next game. Doesn't matter if it's Drakes or Foxes, we'll be better." Morgan laughed as he named other teams still fighting to move to the next round. The Dingoes would play one of the teams for the semifinal. "Sounds crazy, but I have faith."

"Do they have any idea what you escaped?"

"Only the PR lady. Gary and I looped her in right away, in case Burke did what he threatened to do. She has been awesome, and so has Gary. I'm sure she told management, because that's kinda her job, but I feel protected, you know? The coach is good. He's a decent guy, and the team has only good things to say about him. Bodes well, you know? I haven't seen the GM, but I understand the current one is retiring and a new guy's already been hired. Hopefully the new GM won't be put off me, but as long as I'm playing well, I trust it'll be a nonissue."

Marshall bit his tongue mentally. *I can't give my deal away yet.* While he'd like to reassure Morgan, he needed the team owner to sign on the dotted line. "I'm glad you've got Gary to back you up. He turned into a momma bear where you're concerned."

"He's a good one to have in my corner." Morgan finished his beer, something Marshall realized he'd never seen him do before.

He shoved his hand out, ready to put the conversation behind him, and Morgan studied it for a moment before laughing. Then Marshall found himself engulfed in a hug that surprised him with its tightness and length. The strength in Morgan felt good, like something he needed.

Then that something shifted, and the embrace gave way to need. Marshall's hand found Morgan's jaw, gentle but firm as he turned his face so his mouth met Marshall's. The beginning of their kiss was hungry, desperate, filled with the scrape of teeth and beards. Bodies coming together in a collision of pent-up want and shared secrets.

Morgan fisted Marshall's shirt in both hands, pulling him closer for a heartbeat, the taste of beer and victory mingling on their tongues. Heat bloomed between them, Marshall's pulse thundering as he felt Morgan's solid chest press against his, the rink's chill forgotten in the alcove's dim warmth. It was like skating onto open ice. Free and exhilarating, but edged with danger.

Morgan pulled back first, eyes wide, breath ragged. Their foreheads rested together for a moment, exhalations mingling in the narrow space. "I can't. Not now. I'm barely on my feet." He ran a hand through his hair, his fingers trembling slightly. "Jesus. This is a disaster. Please, don't be mad, but something like this would mess up my game, Coach." His chin dropped. "Hockey is all I have. I can't mess it up."

Marshall's thumb lingered on Morgan's jaw, tracing the line of his beard softly before dropping away. Inside him restraint warred with the depth of his want. He liked the pull, the way Morgan's toughness mirrored his own past struggles, making this inevitable. "You won't," Marshall promised, voice low and rough. "I get it. I'm in the same position. I'm sorry, Morgan. I know how you feel. I've been where you are, hiding, afraid of what comes next. Just remember you're not alone in this."

Morgan's eyes searched his, a flicker of longing cutting through the fear. He placed a hand on Marshall's chest as if feeling the steady thump of his heart beneath the fabric. "That means more than you know." The touch lingered, electric, heat remaining even when Morgan stepped back.

Morgan nodded and turned, slipping away, and Marshall knew they were both skating on thin ice.

***

Before their next game, Marshall walked the arena's concourse, the smell of popcorn and beer thick in the air. He paused at a vendor selling team merchandise and picked up a keychain with the suburban team's logo, a snarling dingo. It reminded him of Morgan's quiet ferocity. He paid, then slipped it into his pocket, the metal cool against his fingers.

Fans bustled past, kids waving foam fingers, their excitement a stark contrast to the weight in his chest. He headed to the box, the keychain a small, secret tether to the man he couldn't stop thinking about.

CHAPTER EIGHT

Morgan

Morgan sat in his new therapist's office, a cozy room in a suburb far from Burke's reach.

Dr. Sanchez leaned forward, her pen poised. "Tell me about the game," she said.

Morgan shifted, the memory of Marshall's kiss burning hotter than his goal that night. "It felt...good. Free. Like hockey is supposed to be. But then afterward, Coach...I mean Coach Marshall was there, and it's messy."

"Messy how?" Dr. Sanchez's voice was calm, pulling him deeper.

His voice dropped in volume, becoming a harsh whisper, "It was a catastrophe, really. I can't be out, not as a player. Not intentionally. I know Burke could still ignore the nondisclosure he signed." *For fifty thousand dollars. I hadn't worried he'd hold out for more until Gary told me it was done. Woulda been cheap at twice the price.*

Morgan's hands tightened. "And Coach Marshall is just...Marshall. It's not that the shock of the trade that could still mess up my game. Things are so much better where I am now. But with Marshall, it feels like he sees me, really sees me, and that truly scares the shit out of me." Flashbacks spilled out. "Before my dad died, I hated the way he dealt with me because he knew I was 'soft.' I wake up with his voice in my head sometimes. I always wake up just before I escape. I dream of Burke also, of his fists. Plus there's the ever-present fear of losing hockey."

"Because all of that involves external stressors." Dr. Sanchez nodded, guiding him to name the fear.

"I'm afraid of losing control of *my* life again."

"But you're taking ownership back," she said. "Every day a little more. I'm here, you've got others behind you, and we'll do it one step at a time. You set the pace, you decide who you pull into your inner circle. You've got this, Morgan."

Back at the rink that afternoon, Morgan pushed through his fears during in a quiet moment in the locker room. He glanced over at Jake, who had been the friendliest Dingo and seemed to want to be a friend. They'd had a conversation a few days ago that indicated Jake was at least an ally. Morgan didn't know if the pressure he felt to tell someone else his truth was because so many people knew about his sexuality now, or if Jake just exuded trustworthiness, but he made the decision to confide two powerful secrets. Things that could derail everything he'd worked for in the wrong hands. But this? This felt right. They'd been talking about various coaches and players they had in common, and the need to confide in Jake welled up fiercely.

Morgan whispered, "It's not someone you'd know, but my ex...wasn't...*he* wasn't a nice guy. The bruises I had when I first got here, they were from him. I've got a lawyer involved, but I worry about seeing him again."

Jake's jaw tightened, but his hand on Morgan's shoulder was steady. "You're one of us now. We got you. No matter what. You're a Dingo, and Dingoes look out for their own." Jake lifted a fist for a bump, and Morgan took what felt like the first breath in a hundred years. "Does your agent know?"

"Yeah, Gary knows. So does Ellis in PR. That's all. I've kept my secrets close to the chest, you know?"

"You don't have to keep secrets from me. I've got your back."

The words loosened something in Morgan's chest, a knot he hadn't known was there. He turned to face his locker and ducked his head, hiding the wetness in his eyes. He had to clear his throat a couple of times before he could speak. "Thanks, man."

That right there, my first step to taking me back again.

***

On the way back to his room after practice, Morgan stopped at a local deli, the bell jingling as he entered. The counter guy, an older man with a thick accent, recognized him. "Oakson, right? Saw your goal last game! Good look, good stick."

Morgan ducked his head. “Thanks. Can I get a turkey sub, double meat, double cheese?”

“For Oakson, you got it.”

He sat at a corner table and unwrapped the sandwich. The crisp lettuce crunched in his ears when he took a bite. He pulled in a deep, restorative breath, letting the smell of fresh bread help calm his nerves.

A kid at the next table stared in his direction, clutching what looked to be a hockey card. Morgan motioned to it and pulled out a marker. It turned out to be his rookie card, and the kid’s grin as he signed it was a small bright spot in his day. For a moment he felt like just a player, not a secret.

CHAPTER NINE

Marshall

Marshall stayed and watched the playoff game from the management box, his new team fighting for a finals spot. His old team was out, but even without a final offer, he would have come to provide moral support. The PR lady, Ellis, had been a font of information about players and the support staff also.

She's someone whose good side I'll want to stay on.

The buzzer finally sounded the end of the final period, Dingoes coming up with a first game win against the Drakes, who'd beaten out the Foxes yesterday to take their place in this semifinal round. *Three games to go before finals.*

Marshall's phone buzzed before he could leave the box, a cursory glance revealing the final general manager offer from the Dingoes was now a done deal. He'd be moving over the next couple of weeks, the team putting him up in a hotel until he had an apartment. Next game the Dingoes played would be his first in the role of GM.

He found Morgan standing outside the arena, talking to fans over the fence separating them from the players' section. The guy was still hyped from the win, laughter fogging in the surprising chill.

Marshall waited for him to finish signing shirts and programs and stepped forwards only when Morgan turned from the satiated fans towards the parking garage. "Hey, Morgan," he called, pleased in a way he tried to shove down when the kid turned with a big smile.

"Coach." He stuck out his hand, then thought better of it, pulling it back before Marshall could latch on. "Sorry."

"Don't be sorry. I'm not a coach. Not anymore. As of tonight, it's official," Marshall said. "I'm the Dingoes' new GM. New team for me, and just between you and me, a terrifying brand-new role."

Morgan's eyes flashed, each emotion present for just an instant, but Marshall could identify anger, fear, and finally, the one he wanted to see most...want.

"Congrats and everything, but why? You can't..." He shook his head. "Coach, you can't keep saving me. There's nothing here to save me from," Morgan muttered, ducking his chin, and hiding those telling eyes.

"I'm not trying to save anyone," Marshall said, stepping closer. "I'm just here. My deal with the Dingoes was on the table long before your trade. It's a big step up for me, and all along it's felt right to take the offer." Their hands brushed and heat fired up Marshall's spine. He smiled because it felt like a promise of possibility.

"Okay. Well, congratulations. Sounds like a good gig. I guess I'll be seeing you around the rink, then." He grinned. "Until we meet again." Morgan nodded and turned away, heading for the parking garage, but Marshall followed him. The air was cooler here, carrying the faint scent of motor oil.

"Hey, wait up," Marshall called softly.

Morgan paused, turning with a mix of surprise and that flicker of want still in his eyes. "Seriously, congrats again on the GM gig," Morgan said, leaning against side of a truck. "Feels like fate or something, you ending up here."

Marshall stepped closer, the space between them narrowing. "Yeah...it feels right." He reached out, brushing a stray piece of hair from Morgan's forehead, his fingers lingering just a second too long, grazing the shell of his ear. The contact sent a spark through him, and he heard Morgan's breath hitch.

Their gazes locked, the garage's dim lights casting shadows that made the moment intimate and stolen, almost too intense for having shared only a single kiss. Marshall's hand dropped to Morgan's shoulder, and he squeezed gently. "You've got a good thing here with the Dingoes. Don't doubt that."

Morgan swallowed, his gaze dropping to Marshall's lips for a beat before flicking back up. He leaned in slightly, close enough that Marshall could feel the warmth of his exhales, but pulled back just as their noses brushed. "Not quite there yet," Morgan murmured, a small smile tugging at his mouth. "But thanks. For the trade and the support. All of it."

"It was a hard decision, just so you know, but Gary was very much in favor, so I hoped you'd be pleased at the negotiated trade." Marshall nodded, stepping back with effort, his skin still tingling from the near miss. "You can trust me for my support anytime. Go home. Get some rest. You've earned it."

Morgan pushed off the side of the truck and headed down the garage, but he glanced back once, the promise in his eyes clear. Marshall watched him go, the future uncertain, but maybe it could be theirs to face.

On his way back to the hotel, Marshall stopped at a diner. He slid into a booth and, without looking at the menu, ordered pancakes, the smell of syrup and coffee filling him with a sense of nostalgia for his long-past road-game days.

The waitress chatted about the game as she took his order, unaware of his role. "Good win," she said, pouring a mug of coffee and nudging the dish of creamers closer to where he sat.

Marshall nodded, "It was a good game. Three more to the finals."

"Our boys, playing for the Cup." She shook her head. "They come in here sometimes, cutting up a little, but they're our boys, you know?"

He nodded and grinned as she walked away, shouting, “Order up” through the passthrough into the kitchen.

Five minutes later, he cut into the pancakes, the fluffy sweetness a brief escape from the ache of Morgan’s words.

He left a big tip, the fan of bills on the table a small act of control in a night full of unknowns.

CHAPTER TEN

Morgan

Morgan's skates scraped across the slick surface during practice, the smooth rhythm keeping him centered in the moment. This suburban rink already felt like home, its bright lights a stark contrast to the remembered shadows of his former barn.

On Jake's suggestion he'd come out to Riley too. Told him about his past. Not the full story, but enough of it, focusing on the abuse and the deep, still-constant fear of being outed. Jake had been standing shoulder to shoulder with him, and knowing Jake had his back gave him the courage Morgan needed to say the words again.

Riley's response had been a quiet nod and a fist bump, followed by a gruff "Fuck that guy. You're good here." No pity, just loyalty. The reaction had loosened the vise around Morgan's chest even more, letting him breathe just a little deeper.

***

This was his second session picking at the fraying threads of his past with Dr. Sanchez so far. "I want to tell some more of the guys," he said in a rush. "It'll have to feel right in the moment. But I'm still scared. Maybe more scared than I was before. What was I thinking?

What if it gets out? The media, the fans—they're all going to eat me alive."

Dr. Sanchez's calm gaze steadied him. "I think you are incredibly brave, even being willing to work on a strategy for how best to retake the reins of your own life. You're reclaiming your narrative," she said. "Who you tell, and how much—that's your power."

Morgan nodded slowly, the idea settling like a puck in the net. He clasped his hands in front of him, nervously rubbing the tips of his fingers with his thumb.

Dr. Sanchez continued, "Ellis is aware, and she is on guard about any potential issues in the media. She's firmly in your corner. Morgan, it's normal to fear those things we can't control. If your sexuality came out, it *would* mean huge changes in your life. But believe in the people you choose to trust. Believe they are who they say they are. That they are good friends and colleagues who want the best for you."

Later that day he was pounding out a couple of miles at the team's gym when he saw Marshall come into the room. The man's presence was a jolt, his broad frame filling the doorway. Morgan's heart picked up the beat, his pulse quickening as memories of their first kiss flashed through his mind.

"How's it going with the team?" Marshall asked, voice casual but eyes searching.

"Good," Morgan said, adjusting the speed of the treadmill to a slow jog and wiping sweat from his brow. "Real good. So good, I've come out to a couple of the guys on the team, Jake and Riley." He shrugged. "Saying the words aloud was absolutely terrifying, but once it was over, the truth felt good. Especially their reaction, because they're solid. We're a unit, you know? They've really been supportive." He hesitated, then added, "You being here? It's a lot, Coach. I don't know what to do about you. I—" he wiped his face again with the sweat towel. "I have to get things sorted here before I could even ask if you—"

Marshall's jaw tightened, but his voice was soft as he interrupted, "I'm not Coach anymore. Just Marshall or Davies. And I'm not going anywhere. Not unless you tell me to. I will always listen to what you want." He smiled, the expression growing slowly. "And just for the record, I would. Anything. Everything." He exhaled slowly. "I *so* would."

Morgan's throat tightened. He wanted to close the gap, to feel Marshall's hands again, but fear held him back. Instead, he nodded, grabbing his water bottle. "Good to know," he muttered, heading for the showers, Marshall's gaze heavy on his back.

***

Marshall

Marshall leaned against the gym wall, watching Morgan disappear into the locker room. The kid—*no, not a kid, a man*—was unraveling a boatful of fears, one teammate at a time. Morgan's wariness was a vivid reminder that their tentative connection wasn't just about Marshall. Morgan's career, and even more importantly, his safety, hung in the balance.

Back in his office, Marshall continued reviewing contracts, but his mind drifted to his sister. Dottie had never gotten to tell her story, never had a chance to break free.

Morgan was different. Marshall was proud that he was fighting. He might not fight on the ice, but within his personal life, he was fierce. Marshall smiled, but he felt the expression fade when he thought of Burke still out there, a loose thread waiting to snag.

***

Morgan

After practice he drove to a nearby park, needing air. He sat on a bench, the wood worn smooth, watching kids play tag on the grass. His breath came a little easier as he chuckled at their carefree play, so unlike his own childhood, shadowed by his dad's expectations.

He pulled a protein bar from his bag. The wrapper crinkled as he unwrapped it, and he ate slowly, the chocolate melting on his tongue. A jogger waved, likely just mistaking him for another guy. Morgan waved back, the normalcy a quiet gift, a reminder he could be more than his scars.

He pulled out his phone and stared at the contact list for a handful of minutes. Coach was there, and he took a moment to change it to Marshall Davies, the name seeming unfamiliar and odd. "It's his name, asshole." He laughed at talking to himself, then sighed deeply.

Morgan opened the text thread with Marshall, entries from their time with the Geese were filled with offers to pick up teammates, and then, more recently, a short list of texts from Marshall to him that he'd read but not responded to, each asking a version of "are you okay?"

Can you meet for coffee? He studied the short text and then added, *Today if possible.* Then that looked too needy, so he erased all of it. Starting over, he typed, *I'm going to have coffee at the Armenian diner on Foster Ave. in about an hour. In case you wanted to join me.* The diner was close to his apartment, and they had great coffee.

He blew out a sigh before hitting Send. Morgan looked up to see the jogger going back the other direction. And the guy waved at him again, staring him directly in the face. No one he knew. *What if he's someone Burke hired? What if he comes over here right now?*

It took watching the guy run out of sight before his muscles would agree to release tension.

His phone buzzed, and he jumped a mile, fumbling with the device and coming close to dropping it. He saw Marshall had responded.

Great choice for coffee. See you there.

***

Marshall

That evening, Morgan slid into the booth across from him, his frame filling the space, eyes still guarded.

“Hi,” Morgan said, reaching for his coffee mug and turning it right side up, the universal sign to waitresses that coffee was needed.

“Hey, Morgan,” Marshall picked up his own mug and sipped at the dark liquid. “This is a solid choice. I’ve been enjoying their breakfasts all week.”

“But you live back near the lake, right?” The man looked confused, then rolled his eyes. “Duh, that would be a four-hour commute round trip. Of course you’re set up somewhere closer.”

“The hotel around the corner, in fact. I’ll find an apartment soon, but it’s nice having a linen service at my beck and call.” He smiled. “Boring décor, though.”

“Coffee all you need, sugar?” The waitress leaned over the table to fill Morgan’s mug. Marshall offered his mug for a top off. “You need a menu?”

"No menu, thanks. Can I get a Manhattan beef with fries on the side?" He looked at Marshall. "Anything for you?"

"Already ordered the Manhattan." Marshall chuckled. "Bring them out at the same time, no special trips just for me."

"You got it," the waitress said, swiping at the end of their booth with a wet rag. "They'll be out soon." She left, and they both watched her walk away.

Marshall looked at Morgan, "Coach will be glad you're eating. He mentioned the stress of the trade seemed to have you shedding weight."

"He talks to you about players like that?"

"Well, I am responsible for all staff, players included. We are setting up a weekly meeting. Often enough to keep me looped in, but without me being in-his-face micromanaging. GM is a new role for me, and I keep having to rein myself in when it comes to the day-to-day routines of the players and practices." Marshall shrugged. "I've been through this kind of transition before. When I first moved into coaching, it was all I could do to not micromanage the centers, since that was my role on the ice. Someone who'd coached for decades pulled me to the side and explained to me that I was making my centers nervous, which led to them making mistakes and ultimately had the refs kicking them out of the faceoffs, which made them even more anxious. But

I'd set that in motion by expecting them to play exactly like I had."

"Sounds like good advice. But you taking it? That's what makes you a great coach." Morgan ducked his head. "Made you a great coach."

"I think I'll always be a coach, but I need to bury it deep inside me for a while so I don't step on toes here." Marshall caught sight of the waitress coming out with her arms full of plates, and he reached over and moved their coffee mugs out of the way.

"Thanks, sugar." She set the plates down, then took a bottle of ketchup out of her pocket and set it on the table with a dull thud. "Need anything else, just yell at me."

"Everything looks good for me." He cocked an eyebrow at Morgan, who nodded.

"Smells good, too." Morgan flashed a crooked grin at the waitress, and Marshall felt his breath catch in his chest.

He really is an exceptional young man.

They both dug in, eating five or six bites before they slowed enough for talking to be an option.

"I'm trying," Morgan spoke abruptly, picking at his fries. "Trying to find my way through all this. It's hard. But telling the guys, going to therapy, all of it is hard. I mean, talking openly with anyone has been one of the hardest things I've ever done, but it's also working. But you..." He trailed off, meeting Marshall's gaze.

"I'm here," Marshall said, voice low, fingers brushing the top of the table.

Morgan stared at his hand for a moment, then reached over and set his fingers over the top of Marshall's before pulling back. The electric touch was brief, but enough for now.

Morgan's lips twitched, not quite the smile he'd given the waitress, but close. They ate in silence, the clink of forks louder than words, an untroubled peace settling between them.

***

After leaving Morgan nursing a final coffee at the diner, Marshall drove to the nearby YMCA where he'd soon be volunteering. He hauled two duffel bags out of the car and slipped the straps over his shoulders, each filled with gear for the kids' program. He went through the employee entrance and once in the gymnasium was met with loud cheers and laughter. He grinned as he handed the gear over to the volunteer coach.

One teen, all lanky limbs and shy eyes, showed him a sketchbook filled with bright drawings of hockey players, including one with Marshall's old number.

"You're a legend," the kid mumbled.

“Thanks, but that guy was a long time ago. It’s fun to remember, though.” Marshall ruffled his hair, the gesture automatic, and called him over to the equipment room. He grabbed a battle-worn stick back from the grinning coach and signed it with a marker he always seemed to have in his pocket. Marshall handed him the stick.

The kid’s grin lit up the gym, and Marshall carried that warmth with him, a defense against the uncertainty of this attraction to Morgan and the reality of Morgan’s guarded heart.

Chapter Eleven

Morgan

He slid down the bench to make room for the line coming through the door after a shift. He'd be back out there in sixty seconds or less, so he pulled in air quickly, still catching his breath. For this game, the fifth in the semifinals, he'd been bumped up to first line, dragging Thompson with him.

The kid had wanted to argue, but Morgan knew it was just nerves and stopped him before he talked himself out of a good thing.

Thompson leaned against Morgan's side. "Last up and down before it's us again." His eyes were locked on the defensive line skating right now. "Fast pace is killing them. The Drakes, I mean. We're golden."

Morgan stood, ready to swing his leg over the wall. The player he was to replace lifted a hand, calling for Morgan to enter the fray. When the player was about ten feet away and the puck was at the other end of the rink, Morgan dropped his skates to the ice, pushing off strongly.

He heard Thompson behind him, already starting the kind of chirping that often gave him an opportunity to pull a penalty out of the other team. Razz them enough, find a way underneath their skin, and they'd be more likely to swing at you if they were already frustrated. Morgan was more careful, not even liking the possibility of a fight.

The linesman blew his whistle, arm in the air. Icing by the other team, which gave them a faceoff in the Dingoes' attack zone. He took his place in the loose circle of men around the puck drop, trading grins with Thompson. The linesman dropped the little rubber disc, and the two centers fought over it, slapping sticks at skates and ice until the puck squirted out, coming directly towards Morgan.

He acted on instinct, the product of countless hours of practice to take the puck softly against his stick and angle around to shovel it towards where he knew Thompson stood at the corner of the goal. A quick deflection, and the refs were blowing whistles. The arena's celebration horns sat silent because they'd only blow for the home team, the Drakes. During the two games that'd been played here in their barn, the horns hadn't gone off once.

Morgan found himself enveloped with players, and he thudded his helmet against each man's in turn. They skated back to the bench, Thompson in front of Morgan, shouting as their fists connected with each player's down the line. Their own rowdy celebration, no blasts from horns needed.

He sat on the bench, sucking air and water by turns, listening to Thompson regale everyone in earshot with his version of the play that had ended up with the insurance goal. Morgan looked up at the scoreboard and saw himself on the screen. He gave a wave that was greeted with a chorus of boos, and it made him grin wider. The score told the story, and they were up by two now.

From here they'd go to the finals, playing against the Antelope from out west. More travel time meant more exhausted players, but it didn't matter. He'd be playing in the finals for the frigging Cup.

He stood, watching for the signal from the third line defenseman. He swung his legs over the wall, skates already angled for a hard, fast push when they hit the ice. He slipped into a position behind the forward for the other team, who had the puck, and with a quick tip of his stick, banked the puck off the wall and away from his own goalie.

Thompson was right there to pick it up, skating to the centerline before he slapped the goal, intending on dumping it behind the net. Morgan ignored his replacement standing and waiting, deciding in a split second to chase the puck. He caught up to it behind the net and poked it away from the defense on the other team.

Morgan found himself splayed against the glass while the player crosschecked him across the shoulders. He shouted, "You play like a fucking queer," in his ear, and

Morgan felt himself trying to freeze even as his body moved in muscle memory, fighting for possession of the puck.

"And you play like a loser," he told the player, who yelled in frustration.

Morgan skated directly to the bench, finding himself next to Jake, who was also sucking air in ragged breaths. "Great play," Jake said between swigs of water.

Filling his mouth with water, he swished it around and swallowed it. "Thanks."

"Good job not reacting to that asshole," Jake said on an exhale.

Thompson turned to face them. "What asshole?"

"Doesn't matter," Morgan said, "look at the scoreboard and see what's important here. We've got another six minutes, and then we'll be locked in. Let's keep up the pressure."

CHAPTER TWELVE

Morgan

Morgan adjusted his tie, the mirror reflecting a man he barely recognized. There was a beard-softened jaw and eyes that held more hope than fear. He needed to leave soon to make it to the rink on time. The team's press conference that would officially announce Marshall's new job as GM of the Dingoes was scheduled to take place in an hour. Morgan assumed they wanted the information out well ahead of the final games. Morgan wasn't part of the announcement, not formally, but he'd be there in the crowd, watching along with his uninjured teammates.

He'd talked to Ellis yesterday about the possibility of him coming out on his own terms. Not now, not right during a playoff run, but maybe in the offseason. She'd recommended he talk to his coach soon. Now he just needed to find a good time to have a closed-door conversation. Gary was on board, too, and was willing to be in the room if needed.

It felt really good that he had so many people in his corner. Seemed like the first time in a long time he'd had confidence like this.

Morgan stopped at a coffee shop he'd come to enjoy, the frufru kind with chalkboard menus and too-loud obscure indie music. He ordered a latte, the barista's quick smile a small comfort. Sitting by the window, he watched a light rain streak the glass, his reflection blending with the gray outside. He pulled out his phone to scroll through old photos. Him in juniors, and then there were a bunch of him and his U18 team, grinning and carefree. One image in particular caught his eye. It was of him on the ice, mid-shot, alive.

That's the kind of joy worth chasing again.

The team's media room buzzed, reporters jostling for seats. Morgan stood at the back with the rest of the team, arms crossed, as Marshall took the podium. His voice carried, steady and commanding, detailing his vision for the team. It was filled with catch phrases, like "grit, unity, and progress." He'd made no specific mention of any players and absolutely no mention of Morgan, but their eyes locked briefly, a silent thread stretching across the room. Morgan's chest warmed, the fear of exposure quieter now, drowned by what felt a lot like a growing trust—and a whole lotta attraction, but that had to stay ignored for now.

As Marshall wrapped up, a reporter asked about the team's chances for winning the finals and hoisting the Cup for the first time in the team's history.

"We're building something real," Marshall said. "It's all about our coaching staff, and more especially our players, their heart."

Morgan's throat tightened because he knew Marshall meant him too.

Outside, the air was crisp, the parking lot slowly emptying. Morgan lingered by his car, waiting. Marshall appeared, loosening his tie, his broad frame cutting through the late afternoon light that had followed the rain.

"You good?" he asked, voice soft.

"Yeah," Morgan said, surprising himself with the truth. "I'm getting there." He paused, then added, "Thanks for everything."

Marshall's smile was small, warm. "Just doing my job." But when his hand grazed Morgan's arm, it felt like a promise of more.

Morgan drove back to the rink for afternoon skate, the Dingoes' playoff games beginning all over again the next day. As he adjusted his laces, he looked at the ice gleaming under the lights, and he felt the weight of eyes. Not in judgment, but anticipation. His teammates clapped his shoulder, ready to follow his lead.

He stepped onto the ice, stick in hand, and glanced at the stands. Marshall was there, watching, his gaze steady, unwavering. Morgan held it, heart pounding, not with fear but with something new—a bucketful of hope, still so raw and untested. He pushed off, skating into the unknown, their eyes locked until the first puck flew.

CHAPTER THIRTEEN

Morgan

He swung out of the rideshare car, fleeing the questions from the driver who wanted to know if the Antelope were going to "clean your clocks." The resounding answer from Morgan was a "Hell no," which pulled a laugh from the driver. Still, he was glad to have escaped from the interrogation.

He was frazzled and paused briefly just before security would feel the need to engage him. Even their kind pleasantries would be too much right now. He pulled in a deep breath and held it for a few seconds before releasing it in a trickle from his nose. It would have been almost meditative if he weren't standing in the open air between the parking lot and the building.

Better get a move on it before security calls someone about the obviously loony player.

Some nights were like this, where the weight of the game itself pummeled his last set of nerves. He held up a hand, shocked when his palm flattened out without a tremor. His whole body was buzzing, so it was good to find out he'd be able to cosplay a calm player.

He finally took the first step forwards, walking the rest of the distance to the door. It was promptly pulled open by a burly security guard stationed on the outside.

Another security guard waited indoors with a wand. Morgan passed over his badge and waited while his identity was verified—by a man who'd verified his identity for the past several games.

As always, the man tried to apologize for the delay, and as he usually did, Morgan told him it was no big deal. He didn't want to explain that this routine was probably in large part his fault because of Burke. It was good that the team was taking the risks seriously, though.

Instead of the locker room, Morgan made his way to the rink itself, the biting scent of the ice hitting him while he was still a hallway away. He slumped over, elbows propped on the boards. The ice was gleaming and smooth, the stadium seats empty. It would be another two hours before the doors opened to let fans into the building. This time was for players who needed to see the trainers, who wanted to double- and triple-check equipment, and who wanted to avail themselves with the carb-loaded meal provided by the team.

His stomach hadn't been interested in food all day, but he knew he needed to go in and make a plate. Otherwise he'd run out of gas halfway through the first period. He'd always heard cup games were like that, fast and furious, and could quickly show the coaches who'd been slacking on conditioning.

Conditioning was something he had to stay on top of, the trainers echoing Coach's comments about needing to put some weight on his bones. His issue with eating wasn't with food, but some days, every bite came with a reminder of Burke. He didn't know how it had worked out that way, but more than half of the beatings—and hadn't that been hard to admit they were, he'd been minimizing them as discipline until Dr. Sanchez brought it to his attention—had happened around meals.

Bad associations shouldn't make me starve myself. And I don't, I won't—not now that I recognize what's been going on. Thank God for Dr. Sanchez. And for a new team that feels like home. It's hard to recognize the me from just a few weeks ago as the same person I am right now.

He startled when someone scuffed the floor as they pushed past him, and he looked over to see Jake taking nearly the same position.

"Hey," he said, turning to stare out at the gleaming sheet of ice again.

"Yo, Oakkie. How's it hangin'?" Jake grinned. "Isn't that what I'm supposed to ask?"

"Ask what you want. Doesn't mean you're gonna get a response." Morgan twisted his neck to stare at Jake. "And what the hell is that Oakkie thing? Just call me Morgan, man. I don't need a nickname."

"It'll be next year before I can call you Captain. You gotta give me something." Jake was openly laughing now.

"You won't ever be able to call me Captain. That's too obvious, man."

"I'll find a different one, then. A good one. Maybe by the time we're hoisting the Cup."

"From your lips to God's ears."

The deep voice came from behind them, and Morgan's nerves thrilled to hear it. He knew it was Marshall before he ever looked up.

"Hello, sir." Jake stood, back straight.

"Oh, no, he 'sir'd' you." Morgan chuckled at the expression on Marshall's face.

"I can't call him coach."

"No, that's true, but you could have gone with Mr. Davies over 'sir.'"

"Mr. Davies has a preference, if either of you'd like to know." Marshall looked from Jake to Morgan and back. "Just call me Marshall."

"Oh, oh. Martial law under Marshall. I like that one."

"Marshall will be fine, Jake."

“I need to hit the whirlpool before the trainers come looking for me.” Morgan held his fist out, and Marshall gave him a gentle bump. “I saw the Antelope’s bus pulling up as I came in. I’d rather not hear them dissing the home barn. At least not before the game starts.”

“Have you seen their rink? It’s a flashback to the 90s. I’m already working on the playlist for our first away game.” Jake grinned. “It’s gonna be cool.”

“Cool,” Marshall said, his voice uplifting at the end, as if it were a question.

“Yeah, cool, you know. Cool.” Jake held his fist out, and Marshall gave him a more significant bump that had Jake shaking his hand out. “Damn, Marshall, don’t hurt the moneymaker.”

“Tell the trainers that extra minute for the icebag is on me.” Marshall turned sideways, allowing Morgan to slip past him.

“Will do,” Jake said cheerfully, slipping past Marshall too.

They were silent, walking through the hallways that led to the fitness center. But then Jake stopped Morgan with a hand on his arm. “So did Marshall follow you here, or what?”

“What? No. He said the deal for his contract was in the works way before I got traded.” Morgan wrinkled his nose, his stomach taking a downward swoop. “Are people talking?”

“As people do, but now I can clip the little chirping birds’ wings.”

They resumed walking, and the swoop in Morgan’s gut evened out. “Thanks, man.”

“Don’t mention it.”

The door in front of them was propped wide, the loud chatter and mechanical noises overwhelming the music spilling over into the hallway. Morgan found his steps coming a little quicker. He was ready to get into the routine of game night.

Two hours later Morgan sat on the bench in front of his locker, lacing up his skates. From where he sat in the locker room, he could already hear the hum of the crowd. Warmups had gone well, and about half the seats had been filled that early. The Dingoes fans were faithful to the max.

He started on his second skate, fingernail snagging in the fabric of the lace, pulling painfully at the nailbed. Exposing part of the nailbed had been one of Burke’s favorite little punishments. A way to hurt Morgan without giving him trackable injuries. He shook that thought off, bringing his brain back to game night.

A hand landed on his shoulder, and he jumped as he looked up at Riley, the slim, quiet man nearly unrecognizable in his goalie gear.

"Gonna be a good one, Oakkie. I can feel it."

"That's not going to be my nickname." He shook his head. "Nope, I'm unspeaking it from existence right now. Not a nickname kind of name."

"Jake, I told you he wouldn't take it from me either."

Riley clomped past Morgan to his post next to the door. He'd be collecting fist bumps from every player and would be the last one to take the ice. That was his routine, and Morgan, as well as every other superstitious player, would go with the flow.

"Let's get fired up," Greer, the captain, shouted. "Get fired up." The players picked up on the chant, getting louder and louder until the captain pointed to the doorway. "Get out there and let's play hockey."

Standing at the bench for the national anthem, Morgan poked Thompson. "Two dollars says it'll be a two-and-a-half minute song."

"No fuckin' way, man. I've seen him before. We're looking at three minutes, minimum. I'll see your two bucks and raise you two."

"Four bucks, two and a half minutes against your three minutes. Easy money for me." Morgan laughed quietly. "Easy money."

"I don't know who says we're connected at the hip when we play. You won't even look at me when I take your money. Bet." Thompson leaned backwards, propping his shoulder against Morgan's chest. "We don't have a freakie-deakie connection. Not like some people."

"Yeah, not like some people." Morgan straightened and shoved Thompson off. "A little respect, man. It's the national anthem. Watch the clock, man."

He shook his shoulders and settled his pads back into place. The man singing the anthem was going slower than expected, and he shook his shoulders again, settling his pads back into place once more.

"Two minutes fifty seconds. That's right in the middle of our guesses. Double or nothing next game?" Thompson turned, his signature grin splitting his face.

"Yeah, sounds good." Morgan took a seat on the bench and reached for his water bottle. He sprayed a little water on the back of his neck, then took off his helmet and sprayed a little water on his hair. Threading fingers through the wet hair, he shoved it back off his face before jamming the helmet back into place. "Sounds good."

He climbed back to his feet and leaned over the boards, yelling at the center taking his stance on the center dot. “Get the drop, Tucker. Get the drop.”

The puck fell to the ice and as stick blades clacked madly to gain control. The crowd roared, the sound echoed by the players on the bench.

“Getting in the game, Tommy.” He clapped Thompson’s shoulder as he swung over the boards. In two strides he was at full speed, chasing the puck down the wall. *I can do this. We’re going to fucking win.*

***

Morgan slid down the bench, sucking more air than water from his bottle and turning to ask the equipment manager for another. “Parched.” His voice cracked. “Need more than water, probably.”

The equipment manager tossed him a bottle with a tape identification labeling it as electrolytes. Morgan opened the nozzle and upended the bottle, sucking down as much liquid as he could in the next twenty seconds. He slammed the bottle onto the shelf in front of the bench, then climbed to his feet as he watched the play evolve on the ice.

Antoly was waving him onto the ice frantically, and Morgan realized the man had lost one of his skate blades. He still had to wait for the play to move away from the bench area before he could jump over the boards. The instant he felt the ice beneath his skates, he shoved hard, angling to intercept the Antelope forward trying to enter the Dingoes' defensive end.

"Not today," he chirped, swiping the puck away and angling it to where he knew Thompson would be waiting. "That's mine now."

"Fuck you, Oakson." The less than enthusiastic insult failed to land as Morgan grinned at the Antelope forward.

"Awww, you got big feelings?" Thompson skated up on the other side of the forward. "Tell Daddy all about it."

"Fuck both of you."

Morgan stumbled, then fell forwards, only registering that he'd been tripped when he heard the ref's whistle. He flipped around onto his ass, staring at the player who now had a referee hanging onto one arm.

He fumbled his mouthpiece out and called, "Hey, Thompson, I think I chirped him into a penalty."

Thompson gave him a hand up, looking feral as he grinned around his mouthpiece. "Proud of you, little guy."

He and Thompson didn't play special teams, and until this game, it hadn't mattered to either of them. But right now Morgan would have killed to get back out on the ice.

The power play team battled up and down the ice, and the Antelope got one more shot on goal than the Dingos did before the penalty expired.

And that's not the way we want things to go.

On the ice, a battle for the puck broke out in one corner, Thompson and an Antelope defenseman holding it against the wall with their skates and boots. Morgan waited half a stride out, ready to snap up the puck when it spurted out towards him. Racing up the ice with strong strides, he could hear the blades of the defenders chasing him and watched as the Antelope's goalie skated out to the hashmarks, crouching slightly. He flicked the puck from side to side, forehand, backhand, forehand, finally getting the goalie to commit to a direction. Morgan pulled his stick back and slapped the puck into the net, skimming it right over the goalie's shoulder.

"Top-shelf wizard," Thompson crowed as he threw his arms around Morgan.

The other Dingoes crowded around, bumping helmets together. Morgan took his celebratory path in front of the bench, pounding fists with every player. Then he heard the announcer say it was an unassisted goal, which was even better because Thompson immediately tried to argue with the officials, saying that he should get a point out of the deal because he pushed the puck Morgan's way. Sure, it was on the other end of the rink, but he was certain he needed that point.

His next shift had Morgan dishing the puck to their forward, then following him up to the blue line. There he shifted gears, gliding slowly backwards as he watched the play unfold. Two quick strides put him in the open so he could accept a pass. He did a little give-and-go with Thompson, the puck winding back up on his stick. One of their forwards, a little guy who was always faster than any of their opponents expected, was going round the back of the net. Morgan saw an opening and passed the puck hard and fast, the round disc hitting in the middle of the player's tape, and the man used his momentum to spin around, tucking the puck in behind the goalie.

Morgan's arms went up and he skated to where the forward was already in the clinch of two other players. He piled on, shouting through the noise, "That was a fucking great spin-a-rama."

"Great pass, Morgan," Thompson said as he lined up behind Morgan to do another celebratory fly-by of the bench, knocking gloves with each player.

"I got skills," he laughed, skating backwards. He ran into something and turned.

It was one of the Antelope's hulking defensemen, who scowled down at him. "Skills with your mouth, no doubt. Wanna be my cocksucker?"

Morgan stumbled again, and all of a sudden it was as if his feet were a thousand yards away, separate from his mind. *Do I respond? Do I not? Why don't I know what to do? How can I not know how to respond?*

Jake picked up the slack, shoving the player backwards. "Suck your own cock, jerk."

Morgan skated towards the bench, waving frantically for his replacement.

"You okay?" The trainer was behind him, hands hovering over the equipment bags strapped to his body.

"Yeah, just needed a breather." He grabbed the electrolyte bottle and upended it.

Thompson bumped his shoulder as he came off the ice. "We'll shut that asshole's mouth for good."

"Just leave it. The less we react, the less they gain from their efforts." He shrugged, then stood.

Morgan bent and looked down the ice at the play. Thompson stood next to him, bumping their shoulders together. Morgan smiled, the solidarity of this team bolstering him. Dingoes really did protect Dingoes.

"You can't control what the other players will say," Dr. Sanchez said, "but you can decide how you react. And if you even do react. I would encourage you to find your voice, but in a way that lets you reclaim joy."

"Reclaim joy," he muttered, looking up to see Jake staring at him.

"Let's go," Thompson shouted as he barreled over the boards, Morgan right behind him.

The next few minutes were a master class in defensive play paired with offensive. The clack of the puck hitting the ice would be followed by the singing of the ice as a stick blade scooped up the puck and dropped it into the net. The Dingoes scored three goals in less than four minutes, all while not even allowing the Antelope a shot on goal. Morgan stayed on the ice past his shift change, as did Thompson. There were fifteen seconds left in the game, and Morgan had seen the other team's goalie streaking towards the visitor bench.

He lifted the forward's stick and poked the puck away and back, and as if they'd rehearsed it, Thompson was there to collect the puck. He turned and slapped it into the back of the net from the red line. There were less than two seconds remaining, so they had a halfhearted final puck drop, and then the entire team was on the ice.

"We just took game one in the fucking Cup finals," Riley shouted in Morgan's face, his helmet pushed back on his head. "Game fucking one. Next stop is game two. Bring it on."

"You know it," Morgan yelled back, the goal horns still going off endlessly. He looked up and scanned the boxes, easily picking out Marshall's broad frame. He lifted one gloved hand and watched as Marshall waved back.

Morgan turned, stick held high to salute the fans, and skated off the ice. Half an hour later, he was still buzzing with adrenaline. Game one was in the books, and he'd made it through.

CHAPTER FOURTEEN

Morgan

Morgan sank into the soft couch in Dr. Sanchez's cozy suburban office, familiar with the scent of lemon polish used on wooden bookshelves that lined the walls. He'd dusted for her one session when he hadn't been able to sit still. She hadn't minded, and it gave his hands something to do while his mouth was engaged. The clock on the mantel provided a steady rhythm, like a metronome, the sound reminding him that the emotional storm brewing inside him wasn't life or death.

Reminder to myself that I've been through a lot over the past few weeks, I'll take my anchors where I can find them.

He lifted his face to catch the bar of warm sunlight filtering through sheer curtains. No matter his internal dialog, nervousness still plagued him. Morgan's hands fidgeted in his lap, knuckles white as he gripped the edge of a throw pillow.

Dr. Sanchez sat across from him in her usual armchair, her calm voice soothing as always. "Morgan, last session we touched on your father's influence and how you've carried his demonstrated disapproval with you. How have those memories been sitting with you since the game win?"

He exhaled slowly, staring at the floor. "It's…It gets all tangled up. My dad, he always called me 'soft,' like it was the worst thing a kid could be. Hockey was supposed to toughen me up, but if I cried after a bad hit or didn't fight back in practice, he'd lay into me. 'Man up, Morgan. No one's gonna respect a soft boy.'" He shook his head. "Imagine. I'm eight years old and being told that how I felt inside wasn't valid. I know it wasn't fists like Burke, but words…They can cut just as deep. Made me think maybe I deserved to be controlled, you know? Like if I was stronger, Burke wouldn't have…escalated. I know that's not true, but shame doesn't have an expiration date."

Dr. Sanchez nodded gently, her pen scratching softly on her notepad. "And how do you see that pattern in retrospect? Especially when you contrast your father's treatment with Burke's demanding control?"

Morgan's throat tightened, memories flashing through his mind, from the whispered threats echoing his father's disdain, to that last night of Burke's hard grip on his neck in the kitchen.

"It's the same shit. It really is. Dad made me feel like my 'softness' was a weakness, something to hide. Burke preyed on that. He'd say, 'If you were a real man, you'd handle this,' right before…you know. The ribs, the black eyes." He ducked his head, his voice softer when he continued. "The rapes. He made me believe that I let it happen because I was broken. Weak. I know that's not the truth. I'm not weak, never have been. It was just their play, both him and my dad. Their way of keeping me unsure of myself. But now, with Marshall..." He trailed off, cheeks flushing.

"The kiss?" Dr. Sanchez prompted softly, her eyes kind but probing.

"Yeah. Gah. I mean, I've had hookups. Not a lot, but still. And that's how things started with Burke. But with Marshall, after that game, in that dim hallway, it was like I caught fire. The kiss itself was thrilling. The way he touched me, his hand on my jaw, gentle but sure. But terrifying too. What if it turns into control? How will I know if I'm safe with him? What if I let him, or anyone else, you know? What if I let someone in and they see the 'soft' parts and use them against me? I pulled back, told him hockey's all I have. Can't risk messing it up. And that wasn't a lie. Right now, hockey is all I have."

The clock ticked louder in the silence. Dr. Sanchez leaned forwards slightly. "Vulnerability isn't weakness, Morgan. It's strength. The kind your father didn't understand and so couldn't teach you, the same mix of emotions Burke tried to exploit. But look at everything you've done. The things you've accomplished. I don't believe that hockey is everything to you anymore. You've escaped Burke's control and are taking charge of your own future. You're trusting teammates like Jake and Riley. Those may seem like small risks to anyone else, but you've got to know how big they are. You are a hundred percent reclaiming joy on your own terms. Start there, for intimacy or friendships, with Marshall or anyone else. Be willing to let your vulnerability build trust, not fear."

Morgan met her gaze, a spark igniting in his chest and charring the edges of his lingering dread. "Reclaim joy...Yeah. I don't know. I mean, it felt good telling those guys. My teammates. And there was no judgment from them. The only thing they mentioned was finding Burke and beating him up. Like, I know Gary has my back because he's shown me he does. That he can be trusted. Teammates require a different level of trust, but maybe I can build off what I already have with Jake and Riley. Maybe."

There was a discreet ding from the timer on Dr. Sanchez's desk, and he stood as the session ended.

Outside, the air was crisp as Morgan grabbed a rideshare to head to the game. If Dr. Sanchez had asked him now, he would have said he was scared, but resolved.

I'm in charge of my own story. I'm going to keep finding joy.

***

The local bar was buzzing with the Dingoes' post-win energy, the sharp clink of glasses and mugs filling the air alongside the jukebox's classic rock playlist. Tonight's first selection had been Springsteen's "Born to Run," and it was now on repeat, thumping in the background. Dimmed neon lights cast a warm glow around the tall tables and over where the Dingoes sprawled in booths, foam from their beers spilling as they laughed and recounted game highlights.

Jake dominated the banter from the head of the table, waving a half-eaten wing like a conductor's baton. "And then Oakkie here—yeah, sorry, Morgan, I just like the nickname. Anyway, Morgan pokes that puck like it's his ex's bad attitude! Bam, top shelf! Antelope goalie looked like he'd seen a ghost."

Riley, his goalie pads swapped for a casual hoodie, chuckled, slamming his pint down. "Ghost? More like a freight train. You owned that shift, man. Kept my net clean too. We all owe you a beer for that block in the third."

Ewell was a center on the second line, which was the reason he'd picked a chair at their table. He said, "Had to sting, taking it on the boot like that."

Morgan grinned faintly, nursing his ginger ale amid the rowdy toasts, the fizz bubbling against his lips. The team's camaraderie wrapped around him like a warm blanket, easing the raw edges that still lingered from today's therapy session. "Thanks, guys. Thompson's assist was the real magic. We clicked out there. Doing all the clicking."

Thompson, across the table with sauce smeared on his chin, nodded vigorously. "Hell yeah, we did. Like we've been linemates for years. Dingoes protect Dingoes, right?"

Jake leaned in, his voice dropping conspiratorially amid the noise. "Speaking of protecting...Morgan's got something to share. Go on, bud. We're family here."

Sudden terror made Morgan's heart race, the bar's heat abruptly stifling. But Jake was doing exactly what Morgan had asked of him. He knew he'd be unlikely to grow the circle of trust on his own. It'd be easier to hunker down with the two friends he'd made. Still, he wanted more.

He glanced around the small group at Jake's encouraging nod, Riley's steady gaze, Thompson's curious tilt, and Ewell's puzzled expression. They each conveyed a different reaction now. *What's it going to be like once they all really know?*

Taking a breath, he said, "All right, yeah. I'm queer...uh, gay. The closet hasn't been my best friend, and I'm getting tired of hiding myself, but, after the way every one of you welcomed me, after everything, I figured you should know. I have an ex who was a piece of work too. Restraining order and all that. He was an abusive shit. But I'm out of that now."

The table quieted briefly, the jukebox filling the gap. Thompson broke it first, fist-bumping Morgan across the table. "Respect, man. Doesn't change a thing on the ice. You need backup, say the word."

"Word, Morgan. You're a fucking brave man." Ewell shook his head. "Honored you count me in your friend group."

Riley nodded. "Besides, us Dingoes look out for our own. Proud you're one of us."

Jake grinned, raising his glass. "To Morgan, a man who makes a career of kicking ass on and off the ice!"

"Just not with my fists." Morgan laughed.

"Oh my God, I get it now. That makes all the sense now," Thompson blurted. "Sorry, I've just been trying to figure out the whole 'turn the other cheek' thing you do." He mimed zipping his lip. "Not a peep outta me."

Cheers erupted from the pool tables, glasses clinking, the moment of solidarity moving into more game talk.

In the midst of all the laughter, Morgan's phone buzzed. He looked, half hoping it was Marshall, but the contact was Gary. He stepped away, answering amid the bar's din as he made his way outside.

"Gary, did you catch the game? Three points for me. Shakin' and bakin' out there."

"Ah, no. I didn't yet. I'll look up the stats in a minute." He sounded unlike himself, a more somber version of Gary than Morgan had ever spoken to.

He hid his trepidation, clapping back with, "Okay, so if it's not awesome game stats, to what do I owe the pleasure of your voice?"

"Kiddo, bad news. Burke was spotted near your old apartment. He talked to the doorman, which is a violation of the restraining order. Doorman called me, and I called the cops, so the police are aware, but I wanted to be the one to tell you. Don't worry overmuch. Just stay sharp."

Fear spiked, cold sweat prickling Morgan's skin as he was overtaken by a flashback to Burke's cruelty. He glanced through the bar's front window, looking in at the booth filled with his teammates turned friends. That gave him the assurance to temper the fear. "Thanks, Gary. I've got people here." He filled his lungs with air and sighed it back out. "I'm good. I'll go home in a bit. We're out celebrating tonight's big win."

"Okay, Morgan. Just be cautious. Watch yourself. I'll call back if there's anything else." Gary sighed. "We'll talk soon."

"Okay," he said, then shoved the phone into his pocket as soon as Gary had disconnected.

"Okay," he repeated to himself. Outside, under the night sky, stars piercing the dark, Morgan breathed deep. Past fear was a direct contradiction to his present safety, but the team's support held him steady. *Dingoes protect Dingoes.*

Glancing around, he pulled the door open, the loud cacophony of the bar noise blasting through the air. Thompson saw him coming and slid over, giving Morgan the outside seat.

"All okay?" Riley asked, a frown furrowing his forehead. "You're a little white."

"My manager, but he wasn't calling about the game. Seems my ex has been a bad boy and violated the restraining order. If you see me talking to a cop, that'll be what it's about."

"What an asshole." Thompson said. "Dude, we're hockey players. We can take care of him if you want."

Riley and Jake exchanged glances and started laughing.

"What?" Thompson asked.

"Same damn thing we both told him. Let me know if he takes you up on the offer because he shut me down hard." Jake laughed again.

Morgan shook his head. "Y'all are a violent group."

"But we're your group," Thompson said. "You're stuck with us now, you know. Stuck."

"Because we click." Morgan grinned at his friend.

Thompson nodded vigorously, "We click so hard, man. I've never clicked this hard with anyone before."

Jake, Riley, and Ewell all burst out laughing.

***

Morgan paced his new apartment, the suburban night's sounds seeping through a partly open window, through which he could hear crickets chirping and the hum of distant traffic. The dim lamp in his bedroom cast long shadows on the bare walls and over where his duffel sat only partially unpacked in the corner from the last away game.

Gary's warning about Burke had rattled him far more than he'd let on, the pounding of his heart still skipping along like post-game adrenaline refusing to fade. There was only one person he wanted to talk to. *Marshall.*

He tapped on the contact, then pressed the cool phone against his ear.

"Morgan? Everything okay?" Marshall's voice was low, steady, like shelter in the storm.

"Yeah...Well. Actually, no. Gary called. Burke's been lurking around, violating the restraining order. I don't know what he wanted, but I can make some assumptions. He's going to out me, I'm pretty certain. Gary's call scared the shit out of me." Morgan sank onto the bed, rumpling the sheets with his restless movements.

A pause, then Marshall's careful tone came through. "I'm sorry this is happening to you. Are the police involved? Morgan, are you safe?"

"Police are aware of it. I don't know what next steps there are. And I'm...I'm okay, just really rattled. I needed to hear a steady voice." Morgan hesitated, warmth creeping in. "You were my first thought. And on that note, we'll move to a different topic." He paused and Marshall laughed softly. "Game highlight for me was that top-shelf goal. Felt like I was rebuilding myself. Sincerely confidence building, you know?"

Marshall's low chuckle rumbled through the line, sending a shiver down Morgan's spine. "I saw it live, and it's been the clip on all the sports channels all night long. Beauty goal. The whole game, you were electric. I'm proud of you. Not just for the goal, and making my job easier, but because you're determined to push through to whatever comes next."

The words hung in the air, their mutual attraction unspoken but present. It was there in the warmth of Marshall's voice and how Morgan felt his hesitation softening.

"Thanks. Thanks, Marshall. It means a lot coming from you."

"I'm here, Morgan. Whatever you need. No pressure."

Morgan's breath caught, their one and only kiss flashing through his mind, both thrilling and terrifying at the same time. "Want to get some coffee tomorrow morning? Maybe? It's nice talking to you."

"You bet. I'll be at the diner at nine o'clock, feeding my face and fielding calls. You're invited to be part of my usual morning routine."

"Yeah. I'd like that. I'll see you then. Thanks."

Marshall laughed low. "You're welcome."

Morgan hung up, nerves and anticipation mixing. He pulled out his wallet and dug for the hotline card. He remembered making the call, how relieved he'd felt to be believed, and that he could have a safety net if he just took the first step. He stared at the ceiling, feeling the same pull towards something real. Tucking the card back into his wallet like the talisman it had become, he turned towards the bed, ready for morning to come.

Chapter Fifteen

Marshall

The bus rumbled down the highway towards the Antelope's arena, the engine's low growl underscoring the chatter of players swapping stories and card games. Marshall sat near the front, his broad frame wedged into the seat, gaze drifting out the window at passing fields. As coach, traveling with the team was expected, but as GM, it was definitely not the norm, and he felt the weight of the player's gazes on his back.

This trip, he planned on observing far more than participating. Looking around, he was reminded of the many bus trips he'd taken during his career.

On every team, at every level, and in every league, goalies were all alike, a little weird, and entirely obsessed with stretching. The players had to walk around Riley, who, even during this short bus run from hotel to arena, was doing a warmup routine in the aisle.

Assistant Captain Jake had taken charge of keeping things light, continually cracking jokes.

Marshall's gaze kept glancing off Morgan. He was seated in the back, focused on the tablet in front of him. Likely game footage, knowing Morgan.

Marshall's mind wandered to his sister, Dottie. She was on his mind a lot these days. Now he could look back and recognize how she'd been hiding bruises and how she'd lied to protect her boyfriend, her abuser. His team captain. Marshall couldn't fail to see the similarities mirrored by Morgan's journey. Everything with the ex was still too close, and a dire fear of Morgan being hurt fueled Marshall's drive to help.

Help carefully, as it had to be done without overstepping, like the original trade that took Morgan out of Hammond's reach. *I'd do it again in a heartbeat.*

As the team's brand-new GM, defining and adhering to boundaries were crucial. He couldn't risk even the hint of favoritism, especially with his growing feelings. Pride swelled in him at seeing Morgan's improved confidence. How he stood straighter, the way he drove all of the team to be a little sharper during drills at morning practice. But still, worry gnawed.

What if Burke somehow got close enough to hurt Morgan again? He'd already proved a restraining order wasn't worth the paper it was written on. Morgan was a public figure. All professional athletes were. But as far as Marshall could enforce, they'd been careful to keep his privacy protected.

Ellis slid into the seat beside him, her tablet glowing. "Sir, I have an update on Oakson's press release. We've got a solid plan if he goes public offseason. Discreet, controlled. He's got support. A lot of it. It feels like the whole team could rally around him."

"And if he's forced out before then?" It was a risk, as Burke felt like a loose cannon.

She grimaced. "Yes, I've been thinking about that, sir. I've got an alternative plan if that happens. Being forced out would be less than ideal, bringing endless team coverage during an already stressful series. They're playing for the Cup. It doesn't get more stressful than that. But I've got a different press release just in case."

Marshall nodded, voice low when he said, "Good job. Keep me updated. He's come a long way." He sighed. "Make sure he plans on telling the administration before making an announcement. Can't sidestep the brass."

The bus pulled into the arena lot, and players filed out and into the building. It was familiar to them, as they'd already played the Antelopes a couple of games during the regular season. Knowing their way around the building helped in making them more comfortable.

***

Morgan

Marshall was up in the box as the team skated warmups before the game. Morgan thought the whole team looked sharp, like nothing could touch them. His gaze stayed focused, his strides powerful. There was nothing any opposing player could target as a weakness. He accepted a pass from Jake and tossed it over to Ewell, who tried to stuff the puck past Riley.

The goalie crowed with success as he flipped the puck over along the wall. "Can't catch me, I'm the gingerbread man."

Thirty minutes later, the arena was alive with hostile energy, boos raining down from the home crowd as the Dingoes took the ice in preparation for the game.

Morgan was on the starting line, standing ready as the sound of stick slaps echoed off the boards. The puck dropped with a sharp clack, pitched to the other team at center ice. He recognized an opening move for a play the Antelope used a lot, and he skated hard, intercepting a pass in the neutral zone. His skates carved ice as he dumped it deep. The puck ricocheted around the back wall, and Jake was right there to pick it up and score. Adrenaline surged, overriding any remaining dull aches left over from previous games.

But midway through the first period, Morgan had just accepted a pass when an Antelope forward barreled in, hard. The check slammed Morgan into the glass. Pain exploded from his midsection, sharp and familiar, and Morgan sucked in labored breaths that stabbed as he slid down the wall. *"You bring this on yourself."* Burke's shouted words echoed in his head. Morgan pushed himself up, muscled through the blurred vision, but he still missed a key pass. It all seemed to happen in slow motion, the puck slipping past his extended stick, stolen by the Antelope, and them rushing Riley and scoring.

"Fuck." He cleared the ice, landing hard on the bench. His ribs gave a grumbling jab of pain, enough to have his voice catch in his throat. Once that faded, self-blame hit hard. "My fault," he muttered, echoing Burke's taunts.

Jake clapped his shoulder. "Shake it off, man. That was a shitty hit."

Thompson nodded. "Next shift, we turn it."

The game score stalled, with the Dingoes still ahead 4-3. When the buzzer blew, ending the period, Morgan clomped slowly to the locker room, doubting but resolved to fight back.

Intermission in the Dingoes' locker room was a haze of sweaty gear and spraying water bottles, the air thick with the scent of exertion and liniment. Players were slumped on benches, banter cutting through the tension as the coach paced, delivering a fiery pep talk: "We're up by one. Don't let off the fucking gas. We need to maintain that fucking lead. We do that, and we'll shut the Antelope right the fuck down."

Morgan caught his breath beside Riley, goalie's mask off, his face flushed. "Rough shift out there," Riley said quietly, probing gently. "You good?"

Morgan nodded, wiping sweat from his face with the sleeve of his jersey. "Rough year, man, but I'm here now. Teammates like you make it easier."

Riley fist-bumped him. "You've got grit. We can all see it. Let's go grit it out."

His phone buzzed from where it sat on the shelf over his head. He stood and grabbed it to see a text from Marshall.

Just skate like we both know you can. You've got this.

As they headed back out, Morgan felt hope flickering back to life in his gut.

***

Marshall

The hallway past Morgan's assigned hotel room was dim, the fluorescent lights flickering across the worn carpet. The only sounds breaking the late-night stillness were a distant hum from the ice machine and the faint racket of a player's laughter from a room down the hall.

Marshall leaned against the wall outside Morgan's door, his broad frame slightly hunched, hands shoved in his pockets to keep himself from fidgeting. He wasn't sure exactly what his plan was here. The loss in game two weighed heavy, but it was Morgan's slow exit off the ice, clearly in pain, eyes clouded with something deeper than defeat, that had pulled Marshall here.

Morgan opened the door, his silhouette filling the frame before he stepped into the hall. He was back in his team hoodie, the Dingoes logo stretched across his chest. His face was pale under the hallway's dimmed lighting, and the way he held his left arm close screamed lingering pain from that brutal check.

He froze, plainly startled to see Marshall, then exhaled, shoulders sagging. "Hey...Didn't expect you."

"Couldn't sleep," Marshall said, voice low, careful. "Saw you favoring your ribs. You okay?"

Morgan's lips twitched with something that wasn't quite a smile as he leaned against the opposite wall, mirroring Marshall's stance. The space between them felt charged, barely two feet across but heavy with unspoken things. "Ribs are pretty unhappy with me. I took a hit, and it aggravated old stuff." He paused, eyes dropping to the carpet, voice quieter. "But it's not just that. I missed that pass tonight. Let the team down. Feels like—" He swallowed hard, the words catching. "Like Burke holds a large piece of real estate in my head, telling me I fuck everything up. That I'm the reason things go wrong. Logically I know different, but the weight of the fuckup is overwhelming."

Marshall's chest tightened. He wanted to close the gap and pull Morgan into a hug, but he held back, fingers defensively curling tighter in his pockets. "You're not failing anyone," he said, voice steady but warm. "You fought out there, pushed through pain when most guys wouldn't. That miss? One play doesn't define you."

Morgan's gaze flicked up, searching Marshall's face, vulnerable in a way that made Marshall's heart ache. "I know. Like I said, logically I can excuse myself. But you don't get it. It's not just the one play. It's this heaviness in my head. Like I'm still under his thumb, waiting for the next hit. I'm scared I'll screw this up for the team, for myself."

Marshall took a half step forward, instinct overriding caution as he brushed Morgan's arm with his hand. The glancing touch sent a jolt through him, a spark of want he hadn't let himself feel since the kiss he couldn't forget. Morgan's eyes widened, his lips parting as if he might lean in. The air crackled between them, heavy with possibility, their faces inches apart. Marshall's fingers lingered, thumb grazing the sleeve of Morgan's hoodie, the fabric soft under his touch.

But Morgan pulled back, just enough to break the spell, his hand rising to rub the back of his neck. "I can't," he whispered, voice rough. "Not now. Maybe not ever. I need to keep my life together, stay stable. This...us...It would be too much."

Marshall nodded, stepping back, his hand falling to his side. The rejection stung, but he understood Morgan's fear, the need to hold onto something solid when the world felt like it was crumbling.

"I had someone," he said softly, choosing his words with care, mindful of Morgan's fears. "Close family. My sister. She went through something like you did, with someone controlling her, making her feel small. She didn't think she could break free, but she fought, bit by bit. Courage isn't loud, Morgan. It's you showing up, playing through the pain, trusting your team. You're doing that."

Morgan's eyes softened, a flicker of gratitude cutting through the fear. "Marshall, thank you for seeing *me*. For sharing that with me. For not pushing. I don't know what I want. What I *can* want. Not yet."

Marshall nodded, but before he could step away, Morgan closed the gap, wrapping his arms around him in a hug that started tentative but grew firmer. Marshall hesitated only a second before returning it, pulling Morgan close, his broad hands splaying across the supple muscles in his back. The embrace was soothing, nondemanding, and Marshall could feel the tension easing from Morgan's frame, the way every breath steadied against his shoulder.

"You're not defined by one miss or one person," Marshall whispered into his hair, his voice a low rumble. He pressed a gentle kiss to Morgan's temple, chaste but warm, inhaling the faint scent of sweat and shampoo. It wasn't about heat or want. This connection was for comfort, a silent promise of safety.

Morgan lingered in the hold, his hands fisting in Marshall's shirt, the steady thump of his heartbeat a counterpoint to Marshall's own racing one. For a moment, the hallway faded, and it was just them—two men navigating pain and possibility.

"You make me feel like I could be whole again," Morgan murmured against his neck.

Marshall's restraint held, but the ache of want twisted in his chest. He pulled back slowly, thumbs brushing Morgan's arms as he did. "You already are. Get some rest. We've got another game in two days, and you've got a bag skate tomorrow morning."

"Aw hell," Morgan groaned. "We lost. Of course it'll be a bag skate." His hand lingered on the door handle, his gaze holding Marshall's for a moment longer. He could see hope and caution all tangled together. Marshall turned, heading to his room, the pressure of his restraint difficult, but necessary. Morgan's strength was a growing flame he'd keep protecting from a distance.

CHAPTER SIXTEEN

Morgan

Game three was a full-on rout, with the Dingoes playing to expectations and Riley earning a shutout as the team kept the Antelope to a big fat zero in their own arena.

They rode the bus to the airport for a quick flight home, everyone dozing in their seats. Morgan had his earbuds in and was watching game footage, focusing on the players that were the Antelope's first line. The more he understood their plays, the easier it was to stifle their attempts to gain momentum.

He looked up and caught Marshall's gaze. Other than the attendant, they were the only two people still awake. He finally had a chance to look his fill. Marshall had lost a little weight since taking the GM job, likely due to stress of a new role. His chest was still broad and looked firm. His arms were still those of a hockey player, filled out in all the right places. With Marshall's coat off, Morgan could see the hint of a tattoo on one bicep, and he immediately vowed to do an internet search to find out what was inked on Marshall's arm.

I could just ask him. He'd probably show me.

That way led to fear.

Morgan ducked his head, breaking the intent locked gaze they'd fallen into.

***

Marshall

He stayed turned around for long minutes, using this quiet time of night travel to let his gaze roam over Morgan's face, his strong jaw underneath the playoff beard. But his face was no longer as gaunt as it had been, the shadows under and around his eyes smaller and lighter. He looked like he was healing, and Marshall took a slow breath.

The idea of Dottie meeting Morgan made him smile. Maybe he and Morgan were both healing.

Chapter Seventeen

Morgan

Morgan stood outside Coach Matheson's office door. He was listening to the faint hum drifting through the hallway from the rink's Zamboni, which was a familiar rhythm that steadied his nerves. His palms were clammy, heart thudding like it did before a critical faceoff, but Ellis's advice from their conversation echoed loudly. *"You've got to tell Coach Matheson. We'll all have to work together to allow you to control your own story."*

He knocked, the sound sharp against the muffled rink noise, and stepped inside when Coach's gruff "Come in" rang out.

The office was a cluttered hockey sanctuary, with old playbooks stacked haphazardly on a worn oak desk, team photos plastered across the walls, and a faded Dingoes pennant pinned above a filing cabinet. Morgan closed the door and sank into a creaky chair opposite Coach Matheson, whose weathered face and salt-and-pepper hair screamed decades of experience. Morgan's fists tightened on his knees, but he took a steadying breath, the kind Dr. Sanchez had taught him to use to tame his fear.

"Coach, I need to tell you a couple of things," Morgan started, voice low but firm, a far cry from the quaver when he'd dialed 911 only weeks ago. "I'm gay. I've stayed in the closet, hidden, because I've been scared it'd mess with my career. So that's the first thing."

"Hell of a lead off. Might as well drop the second bomb."

"Yeah. So, I had a one-night stand, who found out I was deeply closeted, and he moved himself in, spent my money, because he could hold me being closeted over my head. My ex—it's weird to call him that— was a grifter from the start. His name is Burke Hammond, and he was abusive, both emotionally, with the games he played with my head, and...and physically. A lot of it was physical. I finally worked up the courage to get out, and the group that helped me were able to get a restraining order, but it's been rough. All that happened just before my trade here. I'm telling you because I trust this team, and I want to be honest."

Coach Matheson leaned back, chair groaning, his sharp blue eyes studying Morgan, not with judgment, but a weight that felt like recognition. "That's a hell of a load to carry, Oakson," he said, voice gravelly but warm. "Takes guts to say all of that out loud. You've got my word that from my end, I've got discretion locked tight. You're a Dingo, and we protect our own, like Jake's been hammering into everyone."

Morgan's shoulders eased, the knot in his chest loosening. "Thanks, Coach. Means a lot."

The desk phone buzzed, and Coach answered, then put the receiver back down and hit Speaker. "Gary, you're on speaker. Oakson's here. He's been bringing me up to speed. I'm assuming Ellis knows?"

Gary's voice crackled through, steady as ever. "Yup, she's got a plan A and a plan B. All the plans. Morgan, good call looping in Coach. Your contract's solid. There's no loose ends for Burke to exploit. We've got protections in place, and the team's behind you. You're safe to focus on hockey."

Coach asked, "Who on the team knows?"

Morgan pulled in a sharp breath. "Jake. Surprise surprise, right?"

Coach smiled and nodded.

"Thompson, Riley, Ewell. Them and Jake. But I want to tell the team. Do you have any hesitation over me doing that now, rather than after the final win?"

"Not going to lie, there's distinct hesitation, but I trust your judgement as long as you keep Ellis in the loop and trust her to do what she promises. She's clutch when the wrong kind of questions are flying." Coach shrugged. "I do appreciate you telling me before the whole team, though." A sly grin tugged at his lips. "Makes it easier to keep the illusion that I'm in charge."

Morgan nodded, unclenching his fists, fingers tingling as blood flowed back. "Appreciate it, Coach. Gary. Both of you. Thank you. So much." He stood, the rink noise swelling as he opened the door. He felt giddy, as if a heavy weight had been lifted off his chest. He wasn't the terrified man hiding in a bathroom anymore. That had never been him. Not really. Now he knew the truth. He was ready to trust deeper, to lean into the team's loyalty.

***

The suburban rink buzzed with light drills, ice shavings spraying under blades, stick taps echoing like rowdy heartbeats. The Dingoes skated in loose formations, laughter punctuating the crisp air as pucks zipped across the ice. Morgan's skates carved smooth arcs, bruises from the last game tender but his stride lighter, buoyed by the trust and friendships he'd built with Jake, Riley, Ewell, and Thompson. The rink smelled of ozone and sweat, a familiar comfort as he joined a passing drill, snapping a puck to Thompson with a satisfying clack.

At a water break, a few players clustered near the bench, water bottles squirting, breath fogging in the cold. Jake sidled up, his grin mischievous. "Yo, Morgan, you're vibing today. Feeling good enough to share with the boys?"

Morgan's pulse spiked, fear making itself known. Moments like these, he regretted asking Jake to help him tell the team. He shook his head reflexively, but Jake's returning nod was steady, echoing the loyalty from every interaction before, giving Morgan a little more courage.

He glanced at Thompson, who leaned his lanky frame on his stick, and the others, Greer, the captain, and Antoly, the quiet forward. "All right," Morgan said, voice casual but heart racing. "Okay. I'm queer. I've been keeping quiet my whole career, but I hate the hiding. That is scary, but telling anyone like I'm doing now is scarier. I don't feel like I've got as much room to control whether I come out or not. My sexuality makes every complication a thousand times harder to get past. I have an ex who is a real bastard. Blackmailing, physically and emotionally abusive, and controlling. I'm definitely not ready to come out of the closet for everyone, but I'm done hiding from you guys. You're my team. My friends."

The group went quiet, the only sound the faint hum of the cooling system.

Greer broke the silence, his voice soft as he said, "Hell, man, that's real talk. Far as I'm concerned, it doesn't change a thing. For the team, it should be all about how you play. You're a Dingo. Enough said." He offered a fist bump, his glove scuffed from practice.

Jake clapped Morgan's shoulder, spouting his ever-present, "Got your back, Oakson. Always."

Antoly, usually silent, grinned and tossed a puck at Morgan's chest, light but deliberate. "Play hard. Love who you want. We're good."

Laughter rippled again, the drill resuming with pucks flying, Morgan passing to Thompson in a seamless give-

and-go. After the whistle blew, he skated a lap alone, the ice smooth under his blades, his chest lighter than it had been in months. The fear of public exposure lingered. He knew the fans and media were going be brutal to deal with no matter when he came out, but he couldn't imagine what it would be like if his secret slipped out during the playoffs. And he never wanted to have to tell his mom. But the "Dingoes protect Dingoes" pact felt like armor, the whole team solid yet untested against the world outside.

***

Ellis's office was a sharp contrast to the rink's chill. It was a cozy and warm space with PR binders stacked on a sleek desk, team logos emblazoned on the walls, and a coffee mug with "Dingoes Bite!" steaming beside her laptop.

The late afternoon light wove through slanted blinds, scattering heat as Morgan sat across from her, the leather chair creaking under his weight. His fingers tapped the armrest, a mix of empowerment and anxiety churning in his gut. *"Reclaim your narrative."* Dr. Sanchez's words rang in his mind, but the thought of fan backlash tightened his chest.

Ellis leaned forward, her sharp eyes softened by a reassuring smile. "Morgan, we're talking about an offseason coming-out because you want control, right? Here's the plan. I'll help you with a personal essay. I've already picked out the sports outlet we'll partner with. We'll want to actively frame your story, focusing on your strength, your game, and living your truth. We'll pair it with a couple of easy breezy interviews, using vetted reporters only, and last, the very last, a social media rollout to shape the narrative. I would advise you plan on being off social media for a couple of weeks after we go live with that. But ultimately, you call all the shots."

Morgan nodded, swallowing hard. "Sounds good. Scary, though. What if fans turn? Or the media twists everything? Should we talk about the blackmail and abuse?"

"Fans might. And media will follow the clicks and views," Ellis admitted, sipping her coffee, the ceramic clinking softly. "But we've got strategies. We'll have you take a speaking spot at the next couple of pressers. That'll safely highlight your playoff grit and telegraph the team's support. Speaking of, Marshall's all in as GM. He's been clear that you're a priority, on and off the ice." Her tone held a subtle hint, maybe a nod to their connection, but he couldn't read the expression on her face.

He stayed professional even as his cheeks warmed, thinking of Marshall's steady presence and the hallway debrief's near kiss. "He's been solid," he said, voice quiet. "Everyone has."

Ellis grinned. "That's the Dingoes way. We'll prep for pushback, but you've got a family here. And if things break before you're ready, we handle it with a similar plan, just expedited. My goal either way is to protect your privacy. Start small, like maybe a podcast appearance post finals. And I don't think we bring up your ex and that relationship at all. There's a legal trail if the media wants to follow it, but that will paint you as the good guy anyway. No harm, no foul in keeping that side of things out of the official narrative."

"Sounds really good, Ellis. Thank you so much for your help and support."

"My pleasure and my job."

They laughed, and Morgan stood.

As he left, the evening air was cool, the suburban street quiet except for crickets. Morgan pulled out his phone to text Marshall. *Thanks for having my back.* He hit Send, the words simple but heavy with trust. Stepping into the dusk, he felt cautiously optimistic, the weight of his past lighter with each ally in his corner.

Chapter Eighteen

Morgan

Morgan sat on the edge of his new couch, the patter of rain against the apartment's window a relentless drone that matched the unease coiling in his gut. Something had him anxious. The dim lamp on the side table cast a weak glow, its light flickering over the sparse furnishings. After some contemplation, he'd sold nearly every stick of furniture from the old house. Too many terrible memories of Burke on every surface. He'd picked up a new coffee table and had a single hockey poster—of Marshall—tacked to the wall.

His phone buzzed on the cushion beside him, the vibration sharp against the silence, and the screen lit up with an unknown number. He froze in place, a cold prickle running down his spine. *Burke. It's gotta be.* The name alone conjured a flash of memory of a hard fist slamming into his ribs in their old kitchen, the crack of pain, the hissed words, *"You're nothing without me."*

He grabbed the phone, thumb trembling as he opened the voicemail. Burke's voice slithered through, low and repellent. "Morgan, you think that NDA means shit? I need cash. You got me? I get fifty grand more, or I'm selling your little secret to every sports rag in the country. You're not safe, not even with your fancy restraining order. Call me." The message ended with a click, leaving

Morgan's heart racing, his chest tight as if Burke's fists were still pressing against his ribs.

He can't touch me. I got out. I'm stronger now.

But the words felt hollow, his mind spiraling to the fear of being outed, his career shredded by headlines, of once faithful fans turning away like they did in his nightmares. He dialed Gary, pacing the small living room, the rain's rhythm louder now, like a warning.

"Kiddo, you okay?" Gary's voice was steady, cutting through Morgan's panic.

"Burke left a voicemail. Demanding money, threatening to out me. Ignoring the NDA." Morgan's voice cracked, but he forced it to steady. "What do I do?"

"You don't do anything. I'll call the police, talk to the detective that's already investigating his violation of the restraining order. They're taking way too long to decide how to handle him," Gary said. "Calling you? That's another direct violation of the restraining order. They are tracking him, that much we know. I believe you're safe, Morgan, but let me check on something. Be right back." There was silence on the line for a couple of minutes, then Gary returned. "Actually, why don't you go to a hotel for tonight, just to be sure you're good."

Morgan nodded, though Gary couldn't see. "Okay. Yeah. Packing now. Should I call anyone? We have game four tomorrow night."

"I'll ping Ellis and Marshall so they're on guard. Marshall's already talked about improving security even more around the rink. This will probably push him over the edge towards that." Gary sounded very in control, and that made Morgan feel better.

"Okay. I'll text you when I get checked in."

He ended the call and grabbed his duffel from the corner. Working quickly, he shoved in clothes, his wallet, and his tablet. As he did, Morgan felt a surge of resolve. *I'm not that guy hiding in the bathroom anymore. I've got a team, a life.*

The rain pounded harder as he zipped the bag, determination edging out fear as he headed to find safety away from Burke's shadow.

***

The hotel suite felt like stepping into a memory, so many nights of his career spent in unchanging duplicates. The same slightly sagging couch, a creaky bed with a plush mattress, a dresser with chipped veneer, and blackout blinds rattling faintly against the window.

There was distant music from a neighbor's TV drifting through the walls, a soft contrast to the storm outside, its muffled notes blending with the hum of distant traffic. Morgan dropped his duffel, the thud loud in the quiet, and sank onto the bed. He pulled out a small notebook, a habit Dr. Sanchez had suggested, the pen scratching as he wrote.

Last time I was hiding, I was terrified, barely breathing. Burke's fists were all I could see. Now? I'm scared, but I'm not that terrified man anymore.

He traced the words, reflecting on that final escape. God, how his heart had pounded, expecting Burke to burst through the door at any moment. Now, his fear was tempered by all the positive changes in his life. The team, Jake's fist bumps, Riley's loyalty. The way Marshall had become a steady presence. Burke's voicemail still echoed, threatening to unravel everything, but Morgan's pen moved faster.

I've got a team. A future. He doesn't own me.

His phone buzzed, and he jerked as if electrocuted. But it was just Dr. Sanchez, calling to see if he wanted to book an emergency session. "Morgan, Gary filled me in," she said, her voice calm like the ticking clock in her office. "Burke's threat is real, but so is your support system. Lean on your team, Gary, and Marshall. They're your strength now. They'll help you get through this."

Morgan nodded, the pen still in his hand, its weight a small comfort. "I'm trying. Told the coach, and most of my teammates. It's helping for sure. But what if he outs me before I'm ready?"

“Then you face that challenge with people who have your back,” Dr. Sanchez said. “Focus on the things you control. You know what they are. Your game and, always, your truth. You’re reclaiming joy, remember?”

The call ended, and Morgan pulled out the hotline card, its edges worn but that number sharp in his mind. He whispered it aloud, as if he needed to memorize it again, “Hurt No More. Hurt No More.” Fear lingered, but defiance burned brighter as he thought of the next game, the waiting ice. He tucked the notebook away, ready to fight, not just for the Cup but for himself.

***

Marshall

The suite’s sitting room was small, intimate, the couch comfortable looking, with a throw blanket over the back. A warm lamp cast soft light across polished hardwood.

Marshall stood near the door, his eyes searching Morgan’s features as he gently closed it. The rain had stopped, leaving a damp chill outside, but the room felt warm, the faint scent of coffee lingering. Morgan sank onto the couch, shoulders hunched, protecting himself, Marshall presumed, from whatever Burke had said in his voicemail.

“You didn’t have to come,” Morgan said, voice low, but his eyes betrayed the relief he felt.

Marshall sat beside him, careful to keep space between them, his hands clasped to avoid reaching out. "Couldn't not. Gary told me about the voicemail. How are you holding up?"

Morgan's fear came back to the surface, the weight of Burke's threat spilling out in a torrent. "He's demanding money, and if I don't pay up, he's threatening to out me. I'm terrified, Marshall. What if he ruins everything? My career, my life. Everything..." He trailed off, eyes flashing. "I know I need to be focused on the Cup games. And I don't want to give Burke any more power against me, but his threat of blackmail is very real."

Marshall's jaw tightened, but his voice stayed steady. "I understand. I know I told you about my sister who faced outside control like that. I know it's not the same, but...she fought to take her life back, one step at a time. You're doing that, too, Morgan. You're stronger than his threats."

Marshall's eyes met Morgan's, and he could see that his words hit deep. He leaned closer, drawn in by the memory of their single kiss, and Morgan's hand found his, fingers brushing gently. Their lips met in a soft, fleeting caress, restrained, but still charged with need as both men pulled in sharp breaths in reaction. Morgan pulled back first, and Marshall heard his own heart pounding in his ears.

"We can't. Not yet. Playoffs are the focus. They have to be. Hockey's always been my salvation." Morgan's eyes were suspiciously bright, and Marshall reached for his face.

He let his hand linger a moment on Morgan's warm skin before dropping it. "I get it. I'm here, no pressure for anything."

Morgan's phone buzzed. He held it up. "Gary."

He answered the phone and put it on speaker. Gary said, "Good news, kiddo. Burke's been arrested. He was picked up trying to break into your old place. A restraining order violation might not have been worth the police's time, but he was breaking and entering, which they frown on. Apparently he'd stashed something in the apartment and was trying to get it back. Not sure what it was. Hopefully we'll get a judge that takes it all into consideration. Either way, he's off the streets for tonight. You're safe."

"No idea what he could have left behind. Are you sure this is for real? He's in jail?"

"Yes, for real. It's up to you if you stay at the hotel tonight or head back to your own bed."

"I...I think I'll stay here. You'll call if there's anything else?"

"Of course, Morgan. Talk soon."

Tension flooded from Morgan. Marshall could track his taut muscles easing like a skate gliding across smooth, fresh ice. Morgan looked at him, their eyes locking, the promise of a future connection present in the lingering gaze.

Relief sparked something deeper, and Morgan closed the distance, cupping Marshall's cheek as he pulled him into another kiss. This caress started soft, tentative, but deepened quickly, lips parting in invitation, tongues brushing in a slow exploration full of unspoken need. Marshall wrapped his arms around him, one hand threading into Morgan's hair, the other pressing against the small of his back, guiding him closer. Heat built, Marshall's breath quickening as the kiss went on.

Morgan broke it first, pulling back with a gasp, their foreheads resting together. "You make me feel safe," he whispered, his thumb tracing Marshall's jaw. "Like I can breathe again. But slow, okay? I need to stay focused."

Marshall nodded, his breath ragged, thumb grazing Morgan's cheek in return. The rain pattered outside, a soothing backdrop to the charged air. "Slow it is. I'm here for whatever you need." He stole one more quick kiss, light and reassuring, before pulling back.

"Thanks again for coming," Morgan said, voice soft.

Marshall stood and gave his shoulder a squeeze. "Anytime."

They parted, the door clicking shut between them, but the look they shared held hope, a tether to something more.

CHAPTER NINETEEN

Morgan

The Dingoes' home rink pulsed with electric energy for the game, the air thick with the roar of fans stomping in unison, their chants echoing off the rafters like thunder. Flashing lights from the jumbotron swept across the ice and crowd, illuminating banners waving wildly. It had been like that through the whole game, all sixty regulation minutes already behind them. There was a mix of "Chase the Cup" and "Dingoes to the Cup" being shouted as the crowd's frenzy built to a fever pitch.

The scent of popcorn mingled with the crisp chill of the rink. Every breath Morgan took was charged with anticipation. The screaming of his ribs had been relegated to a dull ache, easily ignored, and adrenaline surged through him, overriding any lingering pain like a shot of pure fire.

The puck dropped in overtime, with the game tied 2-2, and every player immediately exploded into motion. Antelope forwards charged hard, their skates carving aggressive lines, but Morgan was locked in, weaving through defenders with the grace of a man reborn. No longer the broken reflection staring back from a cracked bathroom mirror, bloodied and defeated. No, now he was whole, fueled by growth.

This one's for Jake, for his loyalty, he thought as he intercepted a pass, spinning away from a check that grazed his side. *For Riley, keeping the net clean.* He dumped the puck deep, chasing it with Thompson at his flank, their chemistry seamless. All it took was a quick glance or a nod, and they were synchronized like extensions of each other.

In the middle of overtime, Thompson snagged a rebound off the boards at the end of their shift. His stick was a blur as he fired a saucer pass across the neutral zone. Morgan caught it cleanly, the rubber disc settling on his tape like it belonged there.

The crowd's roar grew, lights strobing as he deked left, then right, threading through two Antelope defenders whose sticks slashed futilely at air. His lungs screamed with each stride, but he pushed harder. *This one is for Marshall, seeing me through the dark. For Dr. Sanchez, teaching me how strong I already am.* The goalie crouched, glove high, but Morgan ripped a wrist shot five hole, the puck slipping cleanly underneath those pads designed to deny.

The arena erupted, horns blaring, fans leaping as the Dingoes bench cleared. Morgan pumped his fist, dedicating the game-winner silently to his supporters, the ache in his body a badge of triumph over Burke's shadows. Teammates mobbed him. Jake's helmet thudded against his, Riley's glove pounded his back, and

Thompson grinned ear to ear. "That's our line!" Thompson shouted over the din.

Morgan felt invincible, the Cup no longer a dream but within reach, the ice beneath him a foundation he'd rebuilt himself.

***

Morgan

Morgan sat in Dr. Sanchez's now familiar office, a mug of chamomile tea steaming on the side table for him, the ticking clock a steady counterpoint to his racing thoughts. The high of winning lingered, his body sore but his spirit buoyed.

We're still in the hunt. I feel like it's possible.

"Making that goal felt inevitable," he said, voice steady. "Weaving through those defenders, muscles threatening to cramp, but I didn't stop. It's like what you said before. I need to reclaim joy. Burke took so much, but on the ice, I'm me again."

Dr. Sanchez nodded, her calm gaze encouraging. "You've transformed that pain into strength. The dedication you have to your supporters? Even that is a sign of trust, of healing."

Morgan smiled faintly, the session wrapping. He headed to the locker room, the weight of Burke's arrest a distant echo replaced by pride.

***

Marshall

In his office, Marshall hunched over his laptop, statistic software glowing on the screen with lists of shot percentages, faceoff wins, and ice-time breakdowns from last night's game. But his mind wandered, pride swelling again at Morgan's game-winner, the kid's courage shining through.

He's come so far, he thought, fingers pausing on the keys. Worry still nagged at him even though Burke's arrest was confirmed, but shadows like that didn't vanish overnight. His sister's memory flashed, her quiet fights now urging him to protect without overstepping.

A knock broke his concentration, and he looked up with a smile as Jake and Riley invaded his office. "Wanted to let you know we heard about Oakson's ex's latest antics. That asshole is a total dick, but Morgan's a beast," Jake said, fist-bumping Riley. "Dingoes protect Dingoes, right?"

Marshall laughed at the two men's antics. "Dingoes protect Dingoes, for sure."

"Okay, we've got Oakson's back," Riley confirmed, and both men exited the office with as much energy as they'd entered.

Morgan's story was spreading positively, with strong alliances solidifying. He had a solid support network now.

Marshall nodded, approving. This team truly was family.

***

Morgan

The tension surrounding the first game of the Cup finals was a living thing, the Antelope's home rink a cauldron of unfamiliar noise. The screaming home crowd's boos crashed like waves, while the significant sections of Dingoes distinctive navy-and-gold jerseys in the stands rolled with familiar chants. Overhead, the flashing scoreboard was ticking down seconds, ice spraying in frantic arcs from desperate skates.

The Dingoes clung to a 1-1 tie late in the third, the pace leading every player to leave it all on the ice. Morgan's defensive saves were stonewalling Antelope rushes, his body a shield for Riley.

Antoly threw accurate passes that threaded a needle of defenders to reach their forwards. It felt like their chemistry was a deadly weapon, moving the puck around the rink at will.

He skated alongside Jake, who was playing with a ridiculous amount of determination, carrying the weight of the team as he battled for the puck in every corner. As usual, Thompson was the master of drawing penalties without getting a matching one. Unfortunately, the Dingoes hadn't been able to capitalize on those advantage plays, as the Antelope were playing with a matching fervor.

The buzzer blared, the game extending into yet another sudden death, ramping up the sensory overload. The competing crowds' chants were deafening, overhead lights pulsing, sweat stinging his eyes.

Morgan's legs burned, but he dug deeper, blocking a slap shot that rattled his pads, the puck deflecting wide while the pain grew in his hip. It didn't matter—he got up and skated away with a shouted "Got it!" to Riley, who nodded grimly behind the mask.

In a frantic shift, Antelope pressed, but Morgan read the play. It was a replica of one they'd been successful with before. But his compulsive watching of game video helped telegraph their intent. It would be a cross-ice pass aimed for their best sniper to rip off a one-timer. Morgan dove, stick extended, the critical block sending the puck skittering to Thompson.

Thompson flipped it forward, and Jake corralled it with sheer will, dishing to a streaking Antoly, who buried it top corner. The crowd went silent, and then there was a growing swell of noise from the Dingoes fans who'd made the trip.

We just won the Cup!

Celebrations erupted. Teammates were hugging in a pile on the ice, with gloves, sticks, and helmets flying every direction. Morgan found himself at the center of one group, tears mixing with sweat.

When it was his turn, he lifted the Cup high, the metal gleaming under the arena's bright lights, its weight feeling like a triumph over all of Burke's chains. Amid the chaos, there was a private moment when Marshall pushed through, their hands brushing in a congratulatory clasp, electric, symbolizing shared victory and hope for what lay beyond the rink.

Chapter Twenty

Morgan

The suburban streets of the Dingoes' hometown buzzed with victory, a sea of fans in navy-and-gold jerseys packing the sidewalks, cheering as the championship parade rolled through. Confetti rained down like glittery snow, catching in the sunlight, while team banners fluttered from lampposts.

The air smelled of hot dogs and summer asphalt. Horns were blaring as the open-top bus carrying the team crawled forward, the Cup gleaming at its center. Morgan sat between Jake and Riley, with Thompson sprawled opposite them, and all were grinning under the relief of their triumph.

Fans chanted, "Oak-son! Oak-son!" as Morgan waved, his heart full. The crowd's roar was a living thing, wrapping him in a warmth he hadn't known when he'd been self-isolating from his previous team. There'd never been the sense of belonging that he had now.

They all piled off the bus when it reached the stage set up for the rally, which was little more than a makeshift platform in the town square.

Morgan took the mic, the silver Cup catching the sun beside him. "This is for my teammates," he said, voice steady, echoing the loyalty Jake had shown him. "Jake,

Riley, Thompson—it was you guys who carried me through. Dingoes protect Dingoes, and I'm damn proud to be one."

The crowd erupted, teammates whooping. A kid in a too-big Dingoes jersey pushed against the barricade, thrusting a marker and his shoulder at Morgan. "Sign it, please!" he squeaked, eyes wide. Morgan knelt, scribbling his name over the offered appendage with a grin. He realized that he now felt completely at ease, no longer hiding any part of himself from his friends. "Keep skating, bud," he said, ruffling the kid's hair.

Back on the bus, Jake slung an arm around him. "You're one of us, man. All in." Riley and Thompson nodded, their laughter blending with the parade's din. As confetti swirled, Morgan felt like a true Dingo, Burke's shadow fading under the team's embrace. Future challenges loomed, things he couldn't escape, like public scrutiny amid the planned coming-out—but for now, the Cup and his brothers held him steady.

***

Morgan paced his new apartment, the hardwood creaking under his socks, the space still fairly bare but his. He'd finally finished furnishing it with a bachelor's sense of style, a simple couch, a coffee table, a shelf with hockey memorabilia that included a puck from his first pro goal, and a framed Dingoes roster. An old junior jersey now hung on the wall, its faded number 17 catching the lamplight from behind the glass, a relic from his desperate escape.

His phone felt heavy in his hand, nerves twisting as he dialed his mom. He knew how the call would go, but he felt a sense of obligation to her and wanted to tell her before Ellis began the strategy they'd hammered out for bringing him from the closet into the warmth of the sunshine.

Dr. Sanchez's words about reclaiming his narrative, his story, steeled him, his resolve stronger than the fear that once choked him.

"Mom, it's me," he started, voice firm despite his racing pulse.

"Hello, me, it's your mother." She sounded like she always had, at least since his dad had died.

"Mom, I need to tell you something. It's going to hit the news soon, and I wanted to give you an advance heads-up." He pulled in a hard breath, focusing his gaze at the number on the jersey. "Mom, I'm gay. I've been hiding it all my life, but I'm done with that. I'm done hiding. I'm happy now, accepted by my team and by myself."

Silence stretched, then her voice, soft but strained, came through. "Morgan, I love you, always will. But, you know what the church says. Are you sure? Maybe you could talk to Pastor John—"

"No," Morgan cut in, standing taller, the junior jersey holding his gaze immobile. "This is who I am. I'm not broken, I don't need to be fixed, and I'm not changing. I've got people who see me, all of me, and they understand. I'm surrounded by teammates, and I have a therapist to help me sort out all the anger I still have for Dad. But here, with the team, I'm building something real." His voice softened. "I want you to be part of it, but I won't pretend anymore."

More silence, then she sighed softly, her voice filled with a mix of love and worry. "I'll try, honey. I need to pray, and talk to the pastor. But I'm glad you called me."

It wasn't perfect, but it was enough.

"Okay, Mom. I do love you."

"I'll always love you too."

For now, he disconnected the call and stood staring at his first ever game jersey. That was the beginning of his journey that took him all the way to here.

His phone buzzed with a message from Gary.

Kiddo, great news. Dingoes are offering a three-year extension, better terms than the trade. You're their star now. Take a break. You're safe and secure.

Morgan exhaled, relief flooding him.

Thanks, Gary. That's huge.

He crossed to the jersey and traced the shadowbox's edge. The scared kid who wore that sweater was gone, replaced by a man reclaiming joy, the Cup victory and his truth intertwining like the laces on his skates.

***

The after-hours rink was a quiet haven, dim lights casting soft shadows across the smooth ice, the faint hum of the cooling system the only sound. Morgan stood at the boards, clutching the edge of the door.

Marshall sat in the stands, his silhouette steady, the usual clipboard absent, his presence here personal, not professional.

If I don't do this now, I might never get the courage again.

Morgan skated to center ice, then back to the boards, beckoning Marshall down, initiating this time, quite a shift from his hesitation in the past.

Marshall joined him at the gate through the boards, a small smile playing on his lips. "You sure about this?"

Morgan grinned, grabbed Marshall's hand, and tugged him onto the edge of the ice. Marshall chuckled, steadying himself in street shoes as Morgan glided backward, pulling him along playfully. "Come on, GM. Skate with me. Just for a minute."

The empty rink echoed with their laughter, Morgan's strides smooth, while Marshall shuffled carefully. It turned into a gentle chase, Morgan circling him teasingly until they ended up against the boards, breathless. Morgan leaned in, capturing Marshall's lips in a kiss that started sweet but deepened fast, hands intertwining as tongues met in a slow dance. The cool air contrasted with the heat building between them, Marshall's free hand cupping Morgan's neck, thumb stroking his pulse point.

"I'm ready to try," Morgan murmured against his mouth, pulling back just enough to meet his eyes. "Us. Slow, but real."

Marshall's gaze softened, pressing one more kiss to his lips. "We'll figure it out together." They lingered there, shoulders touching as they stood next to the bench, their intimacy quiet but profound.

Marshall stepped back, respecting the space. "I'll be here," he said, pointing to the stands.

Morgan skated a slow lap. The future loomed with his public coming-out waiting in the wings, complete with media storms and fan reactions, but for now he glided smoothly, each stride a step towards freedom.

Marshall watched, their eyes meeting across the rink, their cautious relationship a promise of new beginnings, open and bright.

EPILOGUE

Marshall

The cabin sat half buried in a late snow, a low rectangle of cedar and stone that Marshall's dad had built with his own hands fifty years ago, back when the world still felt wide enough for second chances.

Inside, the fire hissed and popped, throwing gold across the pine floorboards. Morgan stood by the window, arms folded tight across his chest, watching the last of the daylight bruise itself purple over the ridge. He was still all sharp angles and restless energy, the kind of youth that Marshall knew carried invisible damage.

Marshall marveled at his beauty as he watched Morgan from the doorway to the kitchen while drying his hands on a dishtowel. The quiet in the cabin was comfortable, both of them knowing they were with someone who valued listening more than speaking. He'd found Morgan on his apartment doorstep two days ago, courage held together with duct tape and stubbornness. Marshall hadn't asked questions then; he'd just opened the door of the apartment and asked, "You hungry?"

Morgan had nodded. That was all it took.

After so many weeks in the tense limbo, the silence between them had now started to feel like something alive. Not awkward—not anymore. Just...waiting.

Morgan had jumped at Marshall's invitation to a weekend respite. Marshall had spent weekends and whole summers in this cabin. It was filled with only good memories for him, and he wanted it to be the same space for Morgan too.

"You gonna stand there all night, or you coming to eat?" Marshall asked, voice low the way you talk to spooked kids.

Morgan turned. He'd tidied his beard, but his dark hair, worn long for the playoffs, was still falling in his eyes unless he had a helmet on. It was damp from the shower he'd taken an hour ago. He wore one of Marshall's old flannel shirts, sleeves rolled to the elbow, hem brushing mid-thigh over borrowed sweatpants. He looked swallowed by the fabric, small in a way that made Marshall's chest hurt.

"I'm not hungry," Morgan said, but his stomach betrayed him with a hollow growl.

Marshall lifted an eyebrow. "Liar."

Morgan's mouth twitched in an almost smile. He crossed the room, bare feet silent on the wood, and slid onto the bench at the table. Marshall had made beef stew, thick with carrots and potatoes. He ladled a bowl and set it in front of Morgan, then sat across from him with his own.

They ate without speaking. The only sounds were the fire, the wind rattling the shutters, and the scrape of spoons. Morgan made a show of keeping his eyes on his bowl, but Marshall could feel him watching from under his lashes. Cataloguing. Testing. Wanting.

When the bowls were empty, Marshall stood to clear them. Morgan's hand shot out, fingers closing around Marshall's wrist. Not hard. Just enough to stop him.

"I can do it," Morgan said.

Marshall looked down at where Morgan gripped him and felt something settle in his gut. Those slim fingers, knuckles still scabbed from fighting for the puck along the boards. He nodded. "You can help."

Morgan let go.

They moved around each other in the small kitchen, a careful choreography. Morgan washed; Marshall dried. When the last dish was stacked, Morgan leaned back against the counter, arms crossed again, like armor.

"You don't have to do this, you know. With me," he said suddenly. "I know me and my situation are a lot. An extra lot."

Marshall set the towel down. "You're not extra."

"I don't know what to do. I—" Morgan's voice cracked. He looked away. "It feels like I'm always going to be afraid, Marshall. Burke broke parts of my brain. You don't want this."

Marshall took one step, then another, until he was close enough to see the tremor in Morgan's lower lip. "I like you as you are. I'm not trying to fix you," he said. "I hate that you feel still tied to Burke. But I'm not going anywhere. Even if you don't want me, I'm still here."

Morgan's breath sighed out in a wispy "Why?"

Marshall reached out, slow enough that Morgan could pull away if he'd wanted. He didn't. Marshall's thumb brushed the corner of Morgan's mouth, tracing a faint scar there. "Because you look at me like I'm real," he said. "And it feels like I've been invisible a long time."

Morgan's eyes went wide. Then they fluttered shut. He leaned forward, just an inch, forehead resting against Marshall's collarbone. Marshall's arms came up automatically, wrapping around the younger man's shoulders. Morgan was shaking.

"Hey," Marshall murmured. "I got you."

Morgan made a noise that was half laugh, half sob and buried his face in Marshall's shirt. His hands fisted in the fabric at Marshall's back. Marshall held him like that, one hand stroking the nape of his neck, the other steady between his shoulder blades. Minutes passed. The fire settled into embers.

Eventually, Morgan pulled back just far enough to look up. His cheeks were flushed, eyes bright. “I don’t know how to do this,” he whispered.

“Do what?”

“How to want something. In a healthy way, without it hurting or me being forced to participate. Feels like that piece of me, my desires have been buried for so long. I want, Marshall. But I’m afraid of what my head will do.”

Marshall’s heart cracked open. He cupped Morgan’s face in both hands, thumbs stroking over sharp cheekbones. “Then we go slow,” he said. “We stop if it hurts. We keep going if it doesn’t. And remember, pain isn’t only physical. If something feels off, or brings up painful memories, we stop until we’re both okay.”

Morgan searched his face like he was looking for the lie. Finding none, he nodded.

Marshall leaned in, slow, giving Morgan every chance to turn away. Their lips met in a soft but chaste caress. Just pressure. Morgan exhaled shakily against his mouth.

Marshall pulled back an inch. “Okay?” he asked.

Morgan nodded, looking frantic. “Again.”

This time, Morgan kissed him, at first tentative, then hungry. His hands slid up Marshall’s chest, slowly moving over his skin until they wrapped over his shoulders, fingers curling into the hair at his nape with a slight tug.

Marshall let him lead, let him explore the shape of the kiss, the scrape of beard, the warmth of breath. When Morgan's tongue brushed his lower lip, Marshall opened for him, gentle, coaxing. Morgan tasted like stew and mint toothpaste and something sweet underneath, like hope.

They stumbled across the room until Morgan's knees hit the bench. Marshall caught him, hands on his hips, steadying. Morgan laughed breathlessly, surprised at the near fall, and the sound went straight to Marshall's dick.

"Bedroom," Marshall said against his mouth. "Fire's dying."

Morgan nodded, but he didn't let go. They moved together clumsily, shedding clothes as they went. Flannel shirt buttons popped, and his T-shirt was yanked over Morgan's head. Marshall's thermal was peeled off, revealing his broad chest dusted with silver hair, the faint scars from a life lived for hockey. Morgan traced them like braille.

In the bedroom, moonlight spilled through the window, silvering the quilt. Marshall sat on the edge, pulling Morgan down to straddle his lap. Morgan's sweatpants were tented, the outline of his cock clear against the soft fabric. Marshall's own jeans were uncomfortably tight.

"Look at you," Marshall murmured, hands sliding under the waistband of Morgan's pants, cupping the curve of his ass. Morgan arched into the touch, a soft whine escaping him.

“Off,” Morgan said, tugging at Marshall’s belt. “Want skin.”

They stripped the rest of the way, laughing awkwardly when jeans got stuck on socked feet. Naked, they knelt on the bed, facing each other. Morgan’s cock was slender, flushed pink, curving slightly up. Marshall’s was thicker, heavier, and the head was already slick. Morgan stared, lips parted.

“Can I—” Morgan started, then stopped, cheeks bright red.

“Anything,” Marshall said. “Tell me.”

Morgan crawled forward, pressing their bodies together. Chest to chest. Cock to cock. The first slide of skin on skin drew twin groans. Morgan’s head fell to Marshall’s shoulder.

“Fuck,” he breathed. “That’s—”

“Yeah,” Marshall agreed, voice rough. He wrapped one arm around Morgan’s waist, the other hand tangling in his hair. They rocked together, slow at first, finding a rhythm. The friction was perfect. Hot, velvet drag, precome slicking the way. Morgan’s hips stuttered.

“Like this?” Marshall asked, guiding him.

Morgan nodded, frantic. “Don’t stop.”

They moved faster, breaths hitching. Morgan’s cock slid alongside Marshall’s, trapped between their bellies, the heads bumping with each thrust. Marshall angled his hips, changing the pressure, and Morgan cried out, nails digging into Marshall’s back.

“Marshall. Oh my God.”

“I know,” Marshall soothed. “I’ve got you.”

He shifted them, laying Morgan back against the pillows without breaking contact. Now Marshall hovered over him, one hand braced beside Morgan’s head, the other guiding their cocks together. He frotted slowly, deliberately, watching Morgan’s face, cataloging every expression of passion. Morgan’s eyes squeezed shut, his mouth open. He was flushed and wrecked.

“Look at me,” Marshall said softly.

Morgan’s eyes opened, glassy with pleasure. Marshall leaned down to kiss him hard and filthy, swallowing every moan as they sped up. The slap of skin, the wet slide, the creak of the bedframe were a symphony. Morgan wrapped his legs around Marshall’s waist, heels digging into his ass, urging him nearer.

“Close,” Morgan gasped. “I’m so close, Marshall.”

“Go ahead,” Marshall said, voice strained. “Let me see you.”

Morgan's back arched, a broken cry tearing from his throat as he came, stripes of white painting his stomach, Marshall's cock, and all the space between them. The sight of Morgan undone, being so totally trusting, pushed Marshall over. He buried his face in Morgan's neck, groaning as he spilled, adding to the glorious mess.

They stayed like that, breathing hard, sweat cooling. Marshall rolled to the side, pulling Morgan with him so they stayed tangled. Morgan's face was buried against Marshall's chest, one leg thrown over his hip.

After a minute, Morgan mumbled, "Sticky."

Marshall chuckled. "Shower's down the hall."

Morgan shook his head. "Later." He pressed a kiss to Marshall's collarbone. "Stay."

So they stayed. Marshall reached for the quilt and pulled it over them. Morgan traced idle patterns through the hair on Marshall's chest.

"Hey," Morgan said quietly. "You said slow."

Marshall hummed. "This slow enough?"

Morgan smiled against his skin. "For now."

Much later, when the moon had shifted across the window, Morgan stirred. Marshall was half asleep, arm heavy across Morgan's waist. Morgan wriggled free, sliding down the bed.

Marshall blinked awake as cool air hit his skin. "Morgan?"

"Shh," Morgan said, settling between Marshall's thighs. "Want to taste you."

Marshall's cock twitched, already interested. "You don't have to."

"I want to." Morgan's voice was steady. He wrapped a hand around the base of Marshall's half-hard cock, stroking slowly. "Let me take care of you."

Marshall's protest died as Morgan's tongue flicked out, lapping at the head, tasting the remnants of their earlier release. He hummed, pleased, then took Marshall into his mouth, and the slow, wet heat had Marshall's head falling back against the pillow, a low groan rumbling in his chest.

Morgan was tentative at first, exploring with lips and tongue, learning what made Marshall's hips jerk. When he hollowed his cheeks and sucked, Marshall's hand found his hair, but he was careful to not hold him in place, just touching, connecting. Morgan took him deeper, throat relaxing, nose brushing the silver curls at the base. He pulled off with a gasp, then dove back in, setting a rhythm that had Marshall cursing softly.

"Christ, Morgan."

Morgan pulled off just long enough to grin, lips swollen. "Like that?"

"Don't stop," Marshall growled.

Morgan didn't. He worked Marshall with mouth and hand, the other cupping his balls, rolling gently. When Marshall's thighs started to tremble, Morgan doubled down, taking him to the root and swallowing around him. Marshall came with a shout, hips bucking, spilling down Morgan's throat. Morgan took it all, then crawled back up, kissing Marshall so he could taste himself.

They lay tangled again, Morgan's head on Marshall's chest as his heartbeat slowed.

"You okay?" Marshall asked, voice rough.

Morgan nodded. "More than." He laughed softly, fingertips exploring Marshall's bicep. "Did I ever tell you I wondered about this tattoo for weeks? Maybe months. I saw a shadow underneath your classy dress shirt and couldn't imagine never knowing what it was."

"Were you disappointed when you finally saw it and realized it was just a hockey puck and stick?"

"Nope," he said, popping the P. "Was exactly what I hoped for."

Outside, the wind had died. The cabin was quiet except for their breathing.

Morgan traced the scar on Marshall's ribs again. "Tell me something true," he said.

Marshall thought for a moment. "I built my career on a lie, never living as me," he said. "Thought I'd be alone forever. Then I came out, and you should have seen the people scatter. People I'd counted as friends suddenly weren't taking my calls anymore. I was living as me, but with pain every day. Then you showed up with your busted face and your sad eyes, and I realized holding onto my pain was highly overrated."

Morgan was quiet for a long time. Then he whispered, "I used to think love was a trap. Something people used to hurt you." He pressed a kiss over Marshall's heart. "This doesn't feel like a trap."

"It's not," Marshall said. "It's a door."

Morgan smiled, small and real. "I like doors."

They fell asleep like that, limbs entwined, the quilt pulled high. In the morning, there would be coffee and pancakes, the chore of splitting wood, the slow work of building trust. But for now, there was only the warmth of bodies, the hush of breath, the sweet certainty that neither of them was invisible anymore.

The End

ABOUT THE AUTHOR

Raised in the south, MariaLisa learned about the magic of books at an early age. Every summer, she would spend hours in the local library, devouring books of every genre. Self-described as a book-a-holic, she says "I've always loved to read, but then I discovered writing, and found I adored that, too. For reading...if nothing else is available, I've been known to read the back of the cereal box."

Also by MariaLisa deMora

Shatter the Ice Series

In the ruthless world of professional hockey, where vulnerability can end a career in a heartbeat, two men risk everything for a love that could either save them—or destroy them.

Morgan Oakson is the league's quiet defenseman: talented, stoic, and hiding a dangerous secret. Trapped in an abusive relationship with his controlling boyfriend, he's one brutal hit away from breaking. When a desperate 911 call brings his openly gay coach, Marshall Davies, into his life, Morgan is given one chance to escape the violence behind closed doors.

What begins as survival becomes something deeper. Through the adrenaline of chasing the Cup, the raw work of healing old wounds, and the courage to live openly, Morgan and Marshall build a love strong enough to face grief, public scrutiny, and new threats. Together they create change—mentoring the next generation, launching a #HockeyForAll movement, and proving that the hardest fights aren't always on the ice.

Raw, emotional, and unapologetically queer, the Shatter the Ice trilogy is a sweeping hurt/comfort sports romance that follows one couple's journey from darkness to triumph:

- ***Playing for Keeps*** *– The gripping escape*
- ***One More Face-Off*** *– The hard work of healing*
- ***Beyond the Boards*** *– The legacy they build together*

Heart-pounding hockey action, deep emotional stakes, and a love that refuses to stay hidden. Perfect for fans of hurt/comfort, found family, and stories where love wins the ultimate victory.

Grab your jersey, wrap your stick in Pride tape, and experience the complete Shatter the Ice series—where the bravest plays happen off the ice.

Sunnybrook Cottage Daycare Series

In the charming Pacific Northwest town of Willow Creek, Sunnybrook Cottage Daycare is more than a haven of giggles, glitter, and rainbow doors—it's a sanctuary where innocence meets intrigue. *Wall Street Journal* and *USA Today* bestselling author MariaLisa deMora weaves heartwarming cozy mysteries around Theresa Daye-Reed, devoted daycare owner, foster (and soon adoptive) mom to Emily, fiancé (and then wife) to charming librarian Alex, and guardian of pint-sized dreamers.

From **Daycare Dangers** (Book 1), where cryptic kid quips expose corporate murder and family secrets, to **Daycare Shadows** (Book 2), where haunting drawings reveal trauma and hidden estates, to **Daycare Whispers** (Book 3), where faint murmurs and prophetic sketches unearth generational echoes—the series balances light suspense with profound emotional healing.

Each story celebrates found family, protector shadows, big-sister bonds, pregnancy milestones, and the power of truth to chase away darkness. With hilarious kid quips, sensory gardens, and the iconic Exit Express swing, Theresa navigates threats while nurturing her growing family and community, including the launch of Alex's bookstore, Reed Between the Lines.

Perfect for fans of heartwarming cozies with depth, these tales prove that even in whispering winds, rainbows always win. Join Theresa, Emily, Alex, and the rest of the Sunnybrook crew for stories where hugs heal, crayons conquer, and brighter futures whisper just around the corner.

Discover the series today—where every mystery ends with light.

5-Star Reviews for Daycare Dangers

"I loved the characters, the build up of tension and the wonderful children that provide such a powerful impact...."

~Lynne B

"Grab a cup of coffee, snuggle up on your couch, and settle in for a cozy mystery! This is just a good ole wholesome fantastic read. Teachers are wonderful, and when they set out to scare the monsters away, they are even better! After all, monsters are allergic to the truth!"

~Tracey

"I was highly interested in this theme of daycare, danger, and mystery. MariaLisa kept me on the edge of my seat the entire read. I was waiting for what would happen next with clenched teeth (should have read it with my mouthguard in). In many placed I shouted, "YES!". My heart pounded. I was enthralled. I had tears in my eyes as I tried to explain the story to my husband."

~Gail

Borderline Freaks MC

Rev Up Your Heart with the Borderline Freaks MC – Where Brotherhood Roars Louder Than Thunder!

Strap in for a pulse-pounding ride through the gritty, high-octane world of the Borderline Freaks Motorcycle Club, where loyalty is forged in steel, danger lurks around every bend, and love hits harder than a revved-up Harley. From the acclaimed author MariaLisa deMora comes this addictive four-book series that blends raw MC brotherhood with scorching romance, heartfelt redemption, and edge-of-your-seat action.

In **Service and Sacrifice**, honor the unsung heroes of military life as a veteran's path intersects with the club's unbreakable bonds, reminding us that true freedom comes at a cost – and love can heal the deepest wounds.

Shift gears into **More Than Enough**, where a near-fatal crash leaves one brother questioning his worth, only to discover that the right woman can make even the most damaged soul feel whole again.

Accelerate through **Lack of In-between**, as hidden secrets unravel in a whirlwind of passion and peril, drawing a resilient woman deeper into the club's fierce embrace.

Finally, throttle wide open in **See You in Valhalla**, facing the ultimate test of legacy when loss strikes the heart of the club, forcing new leaders to rise from the ashes and defend what matters most.

Perfect for fans of physical drama laced with steamy, soul-stirring romance, the Borderline Freaks MC series delivers non-stop thrills, complex characters, and happily-ever-afters that will leave you craving more. Grab the complete set today and join the ride because in this club, family isn't just blood...it's everything.

With My Whole Heart Series

Dive into the heartfelt world of the *With My Whole Heart* series, where unconventional families forge unbreakable bonds through love, laughter, and life's unexpected twists. Sweet as pie and twice as delicious, these steamy romantic tales deliver guaranteed happily-ever-afters that will warm your soul and steal your breath.

In ***With My Whole Heart*** (Book 1), meet Jaime, a fierce single mom battling to keep her world afloat, and Connor, a man too busy for love—until fate intervenes. When Jaime becomes the surrogate for Connor's big brother, and Connor steps up as the sperm donor, sparks fly in the most complicated way. What starts as a family favor blossoms into a passionate romance, proving that true love thrives in the messiest of circumstances. Readers rave: "This book has a special place in my heart. I was pulled in from the first words to the last." With a 4.44 average rating on Goodreads, this story of unconditional love and second chances is impossible to put down.

Continue the journey in ***Bet on Us*** (Book 2), where Trent and Jacob's dream of building a family collides with tragedy. When Trent discovers his estranged sister's murder leaves behind a teenage nephew, Jericho—a quiet kid hiding a big secret—the couple steps in as guardians. Amid grief and revelations, Jericho finds strength in his uncles' fierce loyalty, echoing themes of acceptance and love. This sweetly complicated tale expands the beloved family from Book 1, blending romance, resilience, and hope. Earning a stellar 4.66 average rating, fans call it "a lover of romance and heartbreaking stories" must-read.

Perfect for fans of emotional contemporary romance with LGBTQ+ representation, found family vibes, and steamy connections. Whether read as standalones or together, these books remind us that love wins—every time. Grab the series today and fall in love with characters who feel like family!

5-Star Reviews for With My Whole Heart

"This story is such a beautiful story of love, loss, and life. Jamie has lived a hard life as a single mom of Nate who by the way is a genius! Connor lost a part of his soul, and never thought he would find love. I would recommend the heck outta this book, it is such a feel good love story,

~Kindle Reader

"I wish I could give Jaime and Connor more than 5 stars. I wish everyone who loved a sweet, hopeful love story that was slightly complicated would read this. [...] My enjoyment of this book is twofold. 1) It's not a storyline I've read before so it was fresh, and by the end, I was definitely wondering what I would do if I was in Jaime's shoes. 2) It's by a favorite author, she up until now writes exclusively MC and I HOPE this helps her to take another chance and give us something like this again."

~Megan

"This book is why I continue to read romance. Two wonderful characters who are just drawn to one another; in spite of reasons that it might not be for the best that they become a couple. Throw in one heck of a wonderful young boy and a family is created. [...] WITH MY WHOLE HEART is the best among a group so filled to the brim. It's not always easy to find that diamond in the rough, and if you are looking for a warm heart, drama, very little angst, lots of soul, and flawless writing.......look no further."

~C Marie

***5-Star Reviews for* Bet On Us**

1. Review by Anonymous (October 28, 2019)

"This book definitely deserves way more than five stars. The absolute love and devotion between Trent and Jake was just beautiful. Watching their love expand to include their nephew was just profound. They never even hesitated, even though they didn't know he existed. [...] Jericho was a fifteen year old boy who had endured constant abuse from his step father while his mother did little to stop it, though she didn't know about it all. [...] His story is heart rendering and left me in tears on several occasions. The grief he endured and the anger he felt towards his mother was handled perfectly, including the unanswered questions as many endure."

~Anonymous

"This is a story of family and acceptance as much as it is a romance. [...] There are really so many layers to this story that I don't know where go with this review. There is the love between Trent and Jacob, the development of their family, Jericho's coming out and finding acceptance where he was accustomed to scorn, his learning what family should be, him finding his way in his new life and finally finding the love he is so deserving of. I highly recommend this book."

~Kat

"Straight to my heart. I swear I felt it grow two sizes as I read Bet On Us. [...] MariaLisa takes us on a whirlwind ride with Trent and Jacob and their new family member, Jericho, Trent's nephew he knew nothing of until he's faced with being his only living relative after his sister dies. [...] Love, without borders, zero conditions, and in amounts that are unfathomable to Jericho are his future. [...] A story about family, even when they're so new and fresh, love without conditions, life lessons and just finding their way. Heartbreaking and beautiful."

~Megan

ADDITIONAL SERIES AND BOOKS

Please note that books in a series frequently feature characters from additional books within that series. If series books are read out of order, readers will twig to spoilers for the other books, so going back to read the skipped titles won't have the same angsty reveals.

Rebel Wayfarers MC series:

Mica, #1
A Sweet & Merry Christmas, #1.5
Slate, #2
Bear, #3
Jase, #4
Gunny, #5
Mason, #6
Hoss, #7
Harddrive Holidays, #7.5
Duck, #8
Biker Chick Campout, #8.5
Watcher, #9
A Kiss to Keep You, #9.25
Gun Totin' Annie, #9.5
Secret Santa, #9.75
Bones, #10
Gunny's Pups, #10.25
Never Settle, #10.5
Not Even A Mouse, #10.75
Fury, #11
Christmas Doings, #11.25
Gypsy's Lady, #11.5
Cassie, #12
Road Runner's Ride, #12.5

Occupy Yourself band series:

Born Into Trouble, #1
Grace In Motion, #2
What They Say, #3 (TBD)

Neither This, Nor That MC series:

This Is the Route Of Twisted Pain, #1
Treading the Traitor's Path: Out Bad, #2
Shelter My Heart, #3
Trapped by Fate on Reckless Roads, #4
Tarnished Lies and Dead Ends, #5

Rebel Wayfarers crossover stories:

Going Down Easy
No Man's Land
In Search of Solace
Puppy Love
Steel and Swagger

Mayhan Bucklers MC series:

Most Rikki-Tik, #1
Mad Minute, #2
Pucker Factor, #3
Boocoo Dinky Dau, #4

Borderline Freaks MC series:

Service and Sacrifice, #1
More Than Enough, #2
Lack of Inbetween, #3
See You in Valhalla, #4

Alace Sweets series:

Alace Sweets, #1
Seeking Worthy Pursuits, #2
Embarrassment of Monsters, #3
All the Broken Rules, #4

With My Whole Heart series:

With My Whole Heart, #1
Bet On Us, #2

If You Could Change One Thing:
Tangled Fates Stories

There Are Limits, #1
Rules Are Rules, #2
The Gray Zone, #3

Other Books:

Outlaw Heartstrings
Sidetracked Love
Only For You
Hard Focus
Salvaged Parts
Spark of the Lock
Dirty Bitches MC: Season 3

More information available at **mldemora.com**.

www.ingramcontent.com/pod-product-compliance
Lightning Source LLC
Chambersburg PA
CBHW050004070726
47592CB00018B/787

9781971653013